ALSO BY THOMAS PRIDE

Fever

Mercia

The Baron

Wonderful Untouchables

King and Country

Zayed

THOMAS PRIDE

Ucadia Books Company

Published by Ucadia Books Company, a Delaware stock corporation (File Number 6779670) 901 N Market St #705 Wilmington Delaware 19801.
First edition.

Thomas Pride is the pen name and true ancestor of an Australian based philosopher and writer.

ISBN 978-1-64419-005-0

Heroes are not born but made

When Lawrence of Arabia was first released as a feature film in 1962, it captured the worldwide imagination of the public. Now, more than fifty years later, it is time to show the world an even greater story of the extraordinary real life and character of Sheikh Zayed bin Sultan Al Nahyan. An epic story that not only matches every bit the action and adventure of Lawrence of Arabia, but exceeds it and all other great cinema classics in terms of depth of character and storyline.

The story begins in 1926 in Abu Dhabi in the midst of the family crisis of the Al Nahyan and the collapsing pearling business. The narrative continues with the unfolding struggles of a young Zayed trying to survive not only the turmoil but the harsh lessons of the desert and the deep cultural significance of the Bedu tribes. The story continues as Zayed as a young man is faced with confronting the coming politics and rivalry for oil and the very real threat to Abu Dhabi and the greater tribes of the region. The tale culminates with Zayed having to find a way through the crisis to avoid all out war and possible destruction of his people.

Zayed seeks to honour the legacy of a major character of history, not by exaggerating his exploits but honouring his wisdom and the truth of his life.

To every man, woman and child living in the Middle East today, who prays for modern day heroes.

No matter how many buildings, foundations, schools and hospitals we build, or how many bridges we raise, all these are material entities. The real spirit behind progress is the human spirit, the able man with his intellect and capabilities.

Sheikh Zayed bin Sultan Al Nahyan

Chapter 1

Abu Dhabi, 1926

A shimmering heat haze danced across a flat sandy horizon.

"A great Bedu Sheikh once said to me, a man must become three things before he is ready to lead. First he must be a dreamer..."

The haze slowly dissolved into a sparse sprinkling of dirty looking buildings and shacks, devoid of any semblance of greenery.

"Second, he must be a warrior..."

A few wrecked and rotting fishing boats lie exposed on the perfectly white sands hugging the shoreline, while a single shoddy looking jetty reaches out into the ocean, hosting a solitary merchant vessel.

"And third, he must be a poet."

Among the shacks and mud huts, one building stood out (Al Hosn Fort), with its high square mud-brick walls and two watchtowers. In front of the main gate to the fort, were two young boys (Zayed and Masoud) kicking a home-made football to an older boy (Hazza). Hazza kicked the ball and it bounced across the road towards the main gate.

Zayed

"You are hopeless," Masoud yelled.

Both Masoud and Zayed openly guffawed with laughter as Hazza scampered across the dirt road to retrieve the ball. He returned frowning at his friends.

"The ball is uneven," complained Hazza. "No one can kick it straight."

"Stop blaming the ball. You do not know how to kick Hazza," replied the young Zayed.

Zayed grabbed the home-made ball from Hazza and placed it in front of him. With one deft kick he launched the ball randomly once again to the other side of the road. Now Masoud and Hazza are splitting their sides with laughter.

"See," exclaimed Hazza. "I told you."

Zayed ignored the playful taunts and sauntered head down across the dirt road to retrieve the ball. He did not see the approaching dust cloud caused by a group of riders fast approaching the gates. He did not even bother to look up as he took his first step onto the road, only to pause and wipe some dust caught in his eye. Only then did he look up to see the figures of Hazza and Masoud waving at him madly on the other side of the road, at the same time he could feel a vibration rippling through the ground.

Chapter 1

Reflexively Zayed extended his right leg to take his next step only to freeze mid stride as a group of horse riders thundered past him, inches from his face and into the fort. A moment passed and then Zayed dusted himself off and ran across the road to his friends to resume their game.

Inside the fort, the riders dismounted (Saqr and his sons Dhiyab and Rashid and their tribesmen) and withdrew into rooms at the side of the courtyard.

******

Not far from the Al Hosn Fort, along one of the dusty unpaved streets of the town, a British soldier (Sergeant Henley), had stopped in front of a dirty squat building, flying a tattered Union Jack and the flag of the Trucial States. He looked down at a piece of paper attached to an envelope in his left hand and then back at the dilapidated building in front of him.

Still uncertain, he stepped to the left and looked down a gap between the building and an adjacent row of shacks. Sure enough, parked out of direct view was the only motor vehicle he had seen in the whole town.

As Sergeant Henley moved to open the front door, he noticed a dust obscured plaque. He unslung his rifle and set down his duffel bag, before reaching over and brushing off the dust to see the words revealed as *British East India Company Office* in English and Arabic. He wiped off the dust from his hand, grabbed his rifle and duffel bag and opened the door.

Inside, the office was dark and dusty, with sunlight beaming through broken slatted windows, creating a spotlight effect on the side wall and on a filthy ashtray on a desk to the back.

Sgt. Henley dropped his duffel bag and placed his rifle on the side wall, before adjusting the envelope under his left arm. As he continued to survey the room, he realised that in the dim lighting he had completely missed the figure of an old looking Arab Legionnaire (Ahmed), still holding his rifle, until disturbed by the entry of Sgt. Henley.

Ahmed opened his eyes and sprung up from his seat and saluted Sgt. Henley. At the same moment, an arm belonging to Lt. Marsden, who had also been missed by Sgt. Henley, reached out of the darkness at the back of the office to butt out a cigarette into a giant ashtray.

"You're three days late," Lt. Marsden grumbled as Sgt. Henley marched forward to him like a toy soldier in perfect precision and saluted the Lieutenant

Chapter 1

"Don't do that," said Lt. Marsden. "Your not in Damascus."

Sgt. Henley dropped his salute. "Sergeant Henley, reporting sir," handing over the manilla envelope he had been carrying. "My papers," he added.

Marsden waved his hand at Ahmed, then returned his attention to the Sergeant still standing to attention.

"At ease Henley."

Marsden leant forward and offered the Sergeant a cigarette. Henley declined.

"I don't smoke."

"Suit yourself. It is only a matter of time," grinned Marsden, before coughing.

Marsden then lit up another cigarette before getting up from his chair and walking over to a decaying map on the wall with the title in English and Arabic saying "Trucial States" and with a red circle drawn around Abu Dhabi. Marsden signalled for Henley to come over and look at the map.

"This is Abu Dhabi," said Lt Marsden, pointing to a small dot on the map. "It was hell at the best of times. Now with the Pearling business gone there is no work."

Marsden paused to puff on his cigarette. "So you see the only entertainment around here is the locals shooting at one another. Smoking is about one of the only things you can do to keep sane."

Marsden walked back to his filthy desk and to a coat stand behind it, where was hung a gun belt, jacket and leather military straps. Marsden grabbed the gun belt and snapped it on and then put on his jacket. He turned and looked at Henley, and asked him in Arabic, "How is your Arabic?"

Sgt. Henley smiled and replied in Arabic, "I was the best of my class."

"Good. Good," replied Marsden in English. "And your aim?"

Marsden pointed to the revolver side arm of Henley. Henley looked down at his revolver and touched the outside leather with his palm.

"A solid shot sir."

"Good. Excellent," said Marsden. "Then say nothing and do nothing and maybe you too will get out of here alive in a couple of years or even before, if this shanty town finally collapses."

Marsden finished connecting the leather strap to his belt and then grabbed his hat and stepped over to the door, causing Ahmed once again to spring to attention.

Chapter 1

"This is Ahmed on loan from the Arab Legion," said Marsden as he pointed to Ahmed. "Ahmed you wait here, OK?" Ahmed nodded and sat back down, as Marsden opened the office front door. "I am taking your new boss to see Sheikh Sultan."

Outside, Marsden walked around the side of the office to the old Packard convertible and signalled for Henley to get in.

"It was originally a gift from the Company to Sheikh Hamdan bin Zayed of the Al Bu Falah," grinned Marsden as he started the car. "There are no real roads to speak of around Abu Dhabi, just a dirty goat track east to the Al Buraimi Oasis. But you have to wait for low tide to get off this bloody island."

Marsden pulled the car out from its hiding place onto the street.

"So why do you have the car?" asked Henley.

"The Al Bu Falah tribe used to own more then 400 Pearling boats but when the business collapsed because of the Japanese and their cultured pearls four years ago, the company repossessed the car and anything else of value it could find."

"Doesn't it anger them you driving up in this car then?"

"Sure it does," laughed Marsden as the car backfired, causing Henley to instinctively duck in his seat, before realising what just happened.

"It's a little temperamental," apologised Marsden. "By the way, those reflexes will go a long way around here."

"Thanks," replied Henley as Marsden pointed to a square mud and stone fort in front of them, rising above the shanty buildings.

"Look, if you are going to survive then you'll need to learn pretty quick that around here it is all about show with these people. Make no mistake, if they see even a hint of weakness, they will slit your throat without even blinking."

Marsden drove the car through the main entrance of the fort, watched by the guards.

"Here we are, Al Hosn Fort," grinned Marsden

"It is so close we could have walked," answered Henley.

Marsden stopped the car in the centre courtyard next to some tribesmen, tending some camels. The car back fires once more, sending everyone ducking for cover and causing the camels to groan before Marsden turned off the car. Two tribesmen move over to the car, before Lt Marsden stands up in the drivers seat and waves a horse whip at them.

"Back. Get back," yelled Marsden in Arabic. "We are here to see Sheikh Sultan bin Zayed. This is my replacement Hansen."

"Henley."

"They don't care," responded Marsden sarcastically.

Marsden and Henley got out of the car and started to walk toward the entrance of the main building of the fort. As they approached to enter the main building, from the side of the courtyard appeared Saqr with a number of his tribesman and his two sons Dhiyab bin Saqr and Rashid bin Saqr.

"Why does the British East India Company honour my brother today?", smiled Saqr.

Marsden bowed slightly to Saqr as his sons and tribesmen surround him.

"I've come to bid farewell to Abu Dhabi and the house of Al Bu Falah your Highness." Marsden pointed to Henley. "My replacement, Henley."

Saqr bowed slightly in acknowledgement to Henley. "Welcome to our humble lands." Saqr pointed to his sons. "These are my sons Dhiyab and Rashid."

Zayed

"I am Honoured to meet you your Royal Highness and your sons," replied Henley in his best Arabic.

Marsden frowned at Henley and whispered, "He's a brother, not the Sheikh."

Henley looked embarrassed at his mistake, as Saqr started to laugh loudly, causing the tribesman and his sons to follow. Soon, nothing but the echo of laughter rang out around the courtyard.

"One day," laughed Saqr. "God willing."

Saqr bowed once more to Henley, only deeper and longer.

"Your Arabic is good British. I apologise for my lack of hospitality, but I must go and attend to matters of business."

A few moments later Saqr, his sons and tribesman disappeared to the side rooms of the fort, as Marsden and Henley swung around and entered the main building.

"Something is up. I can feel it," whispered Marsden as they walked down the main corridor. "Let's just get in and then get out."

"Why?" asked Sgt. Henley. "He seemed like a jovial fellow. It would not be the best diplomacy to wave our hands and then decline their hospitality."

Chapter 1

Marsden nodded to two guards at the end of the first corridor, before heading along a second corridor. Once past the guards, Marsden stopped and whispered to Sgt. Henley.

"Henley. That was Saqr the brother of Sheikh Sultan and his mortal enemy. He still blames the Sheikh for the death of their other brother Hamdan four years ago."

Marsden and Henley nodded at yet more tribal guards.

"Remember the golden rule of the company," whispered Marsden, looking around nervously. "Don't get involved in their politics. It is just business."

"Hello Marsden," a voice sounded from behind them, catching Marsden by surprise.

He turned quickly to see Salmah standing in the corridor, accompanied by her son Zayed.

"Sheikha," replied Marsden as he quickly bowed and then pointed at Henley. "Your Highness let me introduce Henley my replacement."

Sgt. Henley reflexively extended his hand to the Sheikha, before rapidly withdrawing his arm in embarrassment once again in making such a cultural error. Salmah smiled at Henley as Zayed stepped forward, grabbing the hand of Henley and shaking it.

Zayed

"I have learnt to read and write in your language, British," said Zayed, looking very proud of himself. "Have you also come to spy on my father?"

Salmah appeared taken aback and grabbed the arm of Zayed who squealed at the firmness of her grip.

"It is perfectly fine your Highness," replied Henley

"This is Zayed," added Marsden. "The youngest son of the Sheikh."

Marsden looked around nervously, causing Salmah to sense his worry. "Where are your sons and the rest of your tribesmen Sheikha?"

"They have gone on a hunt Marsden. Why do you ask?"

"Because I came across Saqr and his sons Dhiyab and Rashid in the courtyard."

The colour instantly drained from the face of Salmah as she hastily leant down and whispered into the ear of Zayed.

"No," he protested. "I want to stay."

Salmah pressed her grip on the young Zayed, causing another squeal, before he scampered away.

"Go! Go!" yelled Salmah as Zayed disappeared down the corridor.

Chapter 1

As soon as they had lost sight of the boy, Salmah grabbed the arm of Marsden in awkward intimacy, whispering in his ear. "Thank you."

Marsden and Henley watch as Salmah hurried away, before both men finally entered the main hall. Henley looked at Marsden strangely. "What was that all about?"

Sitting at the end of the main hall was Sheikh Sultan Bin Zayed, with his brothers Khalifa Bin Zayed and Mohammad Bin Zayed. Half a dozen guards were standing around the edge of the room, with the women sitting behind a wooden grail to the right side. As Marsden approached the Sheikh looked up and smiled.

"Whatever happens here," whispered Marsden, "keep your wits and don't get involved."

"Your Highness," bellowed Marsden to the Sheikh, "let me present my replacement Henley."

Marsden and Sgt. Henley move forward as the Sheikh stood up to shake first the hand of Marsden and then Henley. At the same time there was a rapidly growing commotion erupting from outside the main hall.

An instant later, there are several loud gun blasts. Henley instinctively pulled out his revolver and ducked down next to Marsden. Sheikh Sultan staggered back, looking down at his left hand covered in blood from his chest. In mere seconds, several more shots ring out.. four, five, seven then ten more shots. Around the edge of the hall, one after another, the tribal guards fall from being shot.

Marsden and Henley watch as Saqr and his sons Dhiyab and Rashid enter into the hall with their tribesmen as young Zayed scurried forward to his dying father, while the screams of the women echo from the back of the main hall.

Saqr stepped up to the Sheikh, now slumped back into his chair, blood covering his robes. "Hello brother," growled Saqr. "This is for Hamdan."

Khalifa bin Zayed jumped up, causing Saqr to instinctively turn and point his gun, until he sees it is Khalifa. Saqr lowered his gun and waved around the room for his men to lower their guns aimed at Khalifa.

"Saqr what have you done!" screamed Khalifa.

"What you refused to do," Saqr snapped back.

Both Saqr and Khalifa pause and look over at the young Zayed sobbing uncontrollably, while embracing the bloody body of his father. Sensing the moment, Marsden got to his feet slowly and composed himself. Saqr looked over at Marsden and brushed his hand at him.

Chapter 1

"This does not concern you British. Go!"

Marsden nodded nervously and started to back away in the direction of the hall entrance, as Saqr focused his attention on the young Zayed in front of him. Saqr turned to one of his tribesman nearby.

"Kill the boy."

As the tribesman of Saqr stepped forward with his gun pointed at Zayed, Henley jumped up shooting the Tribesman dead, before grabbing Zayed and sprinting toward Marsden backing away towards the exit.

In mere moments, chaos erupts. Exposed and in the line of fire as tribesmen take aim at Henley, Marsden drew his revolver. He prepared to fire, first targetting the tribesmen taking aim directly in front of him, while looking for the closest cover.

Marsden got off one shot aimed at a tribesman as Henley passes him, holding Zayed. But the first shot of Marsden missed, and only rattled the tribesmen, causing him to badly miss. Marsden got off another shot, as he leapt for the cover of the table, this time hitting one of the tribesmen in the leg. By this stage multiple bullets whizz closer to him. Marsden fired a third round, as he hit the ground near the table, to see Henley successfully escape the room with Zayed. But a round hit Marsden in his right arm. He recoiled in pain, causing his revolver to spill out of his hand.

"Damn!", yelled Marsden at the pain, as Saqr raised his hand for his men to stop firing.

Saqr stepped forward to Marsden, who was slumped against the wall, gripping his arm in pain.

"Sorry British. You are not badly injured. You should not get involved."

Marsden grimaced as Saqr screamed to his men.

"Get them! Get them!"

In the final corridor to the exit and courtyard, Henley encountered his first deadly threat as two tribesmen holding Salmah aimed their rifles at him and fire, narrowly missing Zayed. Henley calms himself and takes aim at one of the tribesmen, before Salmah breaks free. In the commotion, Henley continues to press forward and took aim, calming himself as he exhaled slowly, before firing his revolver, hitting the first tribesman and then the second.

Salmah, grabbed Zayed and turned to Henley as they rushed to the exit. Bullets whizzed past them, fired by the tribesmen of Saqr who were running down the corridor after them. Now at the exit doors, Henley swung around and slammed them shut, before pointing at the car to Salmah.

Chapter 1

"Get in!"

Henley sprinted over to the car and jumped into the drivers seat, turning the engine over just as two Saqr tribesmen near the gates to the fort take aim and fire. The engine is slow to start, giving the tribesmen enough time to fire a shot that hits the windscreen, causing it to shatter. Then just in time, thick smoke bellowed out of the exhaust, followed by a cracking BOOM of a backfire, causing everyone - including the tribesmen - to drop to the ground.

Henley swung the car around and aimed at the main exit, blocked by the two tribesmen, picking themselves off the ground.

"Hang on!"

Henley tooted the horn as he accelerated the car at full speed and the tribesmen jump out of the way just in time. But by the time the car was fully through the gates and outside in front of the fort, it had begun to wobble dangerously from the acceleration. Henley struggled to keep control as the car fishtailed dangerously close to the ditch running alongside the dirt road.

A few more moments and once the car was out of range from the fort, Henley eased back on the accelerator and traced back the way he drove in with Marsden.

"Turn left here," yelled Salmah, and Henley pulls the car around a tight corner, almost crashing into some tin shacks, before correcting his steering. Henley looked briefly at Salmah leaning forward from the back seat.

"Where are we going?" he asked.

"Watch out!" screamed Salmah, as Henley narrowly misses hitting two old men carrying fishing baskets across the dirt road.

"Follow this street to the end, then cross the sand," she continued. "Get us to Al Buraimi Oasis and Saqr cannot touch us."

At the end of the dirt street Henley stopped the car. He looked in the rear view mirror, spotting a dust cloud approaching from the direction of the fort.

"What are you doing?" cried Salmah, who also looked back at the approaching dust cloud behind them. Henley pointed to the sandbar in front of them, still partially covered in parts by sea water.

"It is blocked," he yelled.

"But they will kill us!" screamed Salmah as Henley looked again in the rear vision mirror to see the figures of a group of horse riders now in the street and the distinct sound of rifle shots.

"Mummy!" cried Zayed, as he looked back at the figure of the approaching riders.

Henley sighed. "Hold on. There is only one way to do this. If we get stuck we're dead."

Once again, Henley floored the accelerator as the car lurched forward gaining more and more speed, before hitting the exposed sandbar and then the water. Yet the water was mercifully shallow at just a few inches deep at the coming low tide. When the car made contact, it merely ploughed through and across the sand bars to the dirt road on the other side, flying past a sign signalling Al Buraimi.

Zayed

Chapter 2

Al Jahili

A small fort (Al Jahili), surrounded by a grove of palms, bathed in the soft afternoon light. The only clue to its occupants being the unmistakable convertible Packard motor vehicle hidden within the palm grove.

Inside the main room of the fort, Henley was seated at a table, cigarette in hand, with young Zayed sitting opposite. In front of him, Salmah was pacing the centre of the room like a caged lioness. Around the edge of the room were her three older sons Shakhbut, Khaled and Hazza.

"No. I forbid it!" she yelled at Shakhbut.

"Woman. I am now head of the family," Shakhbut snapped back defiantly.

Salmah marched forward and slapped Shakhbut across the face. "How dare you raise your voice to me," she yelled.

Shakhbut at first looked stunned, before glaring menacingly at her. As Shakhbut stepped forward, Zayed leapt from his chair and scrambled to stand in his way, with little effect. Shakhbut pushed him out of the way so hard that he hit the side wall with a thud. Salmah was at first shocked, before she focused her gaze on Shakhbut. He quickly scampered away to the edge of the room. Salmah then grabbed Zayed and crouched down to see if he was hurt, glaring back once again at Shakhbut.

"I am your mother. And you are my eldest son. And I shall not have any more of those I love die today or tomorrow because of foolish rage."

"Mother is right Shakh," said Hazza. "We do not know how many men or guns uncle Saqr has now."

Shakhbut glared at Hazza as Khaled nodded his head in agreement.

"I agree with Hazza," added Khaled tentatively.

"This doesn't concern you Khaled," growled Shakhbut. "You can't shoot straight so you are not coming."

"You must wait Shakhbut," pleaded Salmah.

"They did not even let us bury our own father," moaned Shakhbut as Salmah opened her arms and Shakhbut embraced her and started to sob.

"Nor did they let his only wife mourn," she said softly. "The time will come my son. Your uncles will bury him today and soon we will repay the same. But for now, keep guard for the sons of Saqr and tomorrow we shall see Sheikh Ahmad of the Dhawahir and seek his protection."

Chapter 2

Al Jimi

Salmah, Shakhbut, Khaled, Hazza, Zayed and several bodyguards arrive on horses to a small village (Al Jimi). They slow down through the village as the inhabitants eye them suspiciously. They stop at a heavily guarded compound (Al Jimi Fort).

The main gate of the fort was opened by a tall Bedu tribesman (Mahmud), who stared at them and signalled for the group to come inside. They all dismounted then walked into the compound of the Sheikh.

The Bedu tribesmen took hold of the horses as Salmah signals for her sons to follow her into the main area.

Shakhbut, followed by Khaled, then Hazza and finally Zayed and his mother Salmah entered the main hall of the fort. They all come face to face with Sheikh Ahmad who remained seated. All bow, before Salmah withdrew to where the women are sitting behind a large veil cloth dividing the room.

"May God bless you and your people with long life and prosperity," said Shakhbut.

Zayed

The Sheikh signalled for them to sit and the brothers form a line in front of the Sheikh.

"I grieve for the death of your father," said the Sheikh, "and for the blood that continues to be spilt among the Bani Yas since the passing of your grandfather the great Zayed."

"We are honoured by your prayers and our family seeks only to remain in honour and peace with the Dhawahir," bowed Shakhbut

"I hear your words but this may be difficult," said the Sheikh. "Saqr has already sent Rashid and some men to Al Muwaiji Fort."

Hazza stood up and started to speak. "But we-"

Shakhbut put his hand up and cut off Hazza from saying another word.

"I shall deal with Saqr and his sons," interrupted Shakhbut. "But for now, I ask only for your protection."

"In exchange for what?" said the Sheikh. "You have lost Abu Dhabi and Al Muwaiji and soon I fear also Al Jahili Fort as well."

"Shakhbut I do not doubt your courage or your lust for revenge. But what are you prepared to offer in return for my people against the demands of Saqr?"

"Name your price," replied Shakhbut.

Chapter 2

Sheikh Ahmad looked over at the young Zayed and pointed at him.

"Then I shall take Zayed," said the Sheikh.

Salmah sprung up from behind the cloth veil and pushed forward in plain sight of the men.

"NO! He is my son!" yelled Salmah.

Her outburst caused such a commotion that Ibrahim and several other Dhawahir tribesmen leapt forward in outrage. The other women desperately tried to drag Salmah back behind the veil, while she resisted their pulling. The din and yelling rose until above all of it the huge roar of laughter of Sheikh Ahmad cuts through and the tension in the room eases.

"Why does my wife not have such spirit?" laughed Sheikh Ahmad, smiling at Salmah. "Woman I am not stealing your son. I am proposing an insurance for our agreement. I hear he is a very bright mind like his mother and can read and write in English as well as arithmetic."

"What if I do not want to stay?" protested the young Zayed.

Shakhbut looked over at Zayed and pleaded with him to be quiet.

"But why?" Zayed insisted. "Is my life not my own to choose?"

Shakhbut looked back to Sheikh Ahmad and nodded affirmatively.

"Good," smiled Sheikh Ahmad, opening his arms to Zayed. "Come my boy," he added. "I shall teach you the ancient ways of your ancestors and you shall teach my children the ways of the British."

Zayed looked over at the anxious faces of his brothers and then swung around to see the face of his mother, who nodded at him and signalled for him to go to Sheikh Ahmad. The Sheikh embraced Zayed briefly and then gets up, as the rest of the Dhawahir also get up.

Zayed looked back at his mother and then back at the Sheikh.

"Go on then," signalled the Sheikh. "Say your goodbye to your mother."

Sheikh Ahmad moved over to Salmah. "Woman, he will be safe," bowed the Sheikh to Salmah. "This is my word."

Zayed hastened over and hugged his mother. Salmah broke the embrace and then crouched down to eye level with Zayed.

"Be brave my son," she said gently. "We will come for you soon."

Chapter 2

Salmah and Shakhbut and Hazza turn and bow
before leaving the room, with Zayed remaining behind.

Zayed

Chapter 3

Al Hosn Fort

A party of men dressed in traditional bedouin robes (Sheikh Saeed Bin Maktoum and his young son Rashid Bin Saeed with several tribesmen) march along the entrance hallway into the main hall.

Inside the main hall was sitting Saqr, with his two sons Dhiyab bin Saqr and Rashid bin Saqr standing beside him. Around the edge of the room was an array of guards. When Sheikh Saeed Bin Maktoum entered, Saqr jumped up from his chair.

"Cousin. Praise be to God for your visit," smiled Saqr as he embraced Sheikh Saeed Bin Maktoum.

"My Son," said Sheikh Saeed, pointing at Rashid.

Saqr acknowledged Rashid and then directed for Sheikh Saeed and his son to sit down.

"I bring news from the Bani Yas," said Sheikh Saeed Bin Maktoum. "They do not agree with your action involving the British-"

"They involved themselves in our own affairs in contradiction to their assurances," interrupted Saqr. "In any event, they disciplined their own men and have left Abu Dhabi."

Sheikh Saeed Bin Maktoum frowned upon the interruption from Saqr, before continuing.

"As I expressed earlier, they did not approve," said Sheikh Saeed, "but consider the death of Sultan and your position as head of the Al Bu Falah as lawful. The Al Qawasim also agree."

Saqr nodded and smiled. "Cousin, it has been difficult for both our families since the death of our Pearling fleets of Dubai and Abu Dhabi," he said. "How might we find a way to forge even stronger ties to survive these times?"

"My son Rashid is in need of a good wife," replied Sheikh Saeed. "I understand you are now the guardian to Latifa the daughter of Hamdan your brother, may his soul be at peace."

Saqr nodded affirmatively and then signalled to the women behind the grail. "Latifa come forward," he commanded.

From behind the grail came a young girl dressed in a burka.

"I am sure you will be most pleased," said Saqr to Sheikh Saeed. "She is a beautiful young girl with a strong mind."

Sheikh Saaed got up, followed by his son Rashid and they both bowed to Latifa, who nervously acknowledged them before running back to the other women behind the grail.

"Then it is settled. Let the Al Bu Falasah and the Al Bu Falah be united in marriage and we shall find a way to overcome these trials of heaven, God willing," said Sheikh Saeed.

The men embrace and Saqr watches Sheikh Saeed and his son and tribesmen depart.

Dhiyab approached his father. "Father, the sons of Sultan have been granted protection by the Dhawahir Bedu," said Dhiyab Bin Saqr. "Sheikh Ahmad ibn Muhammad is holding Zayed as insurance."

Saqr rubbed his face as he stepped away, then turned around.

"Then let us be patient my son. I shall appoint my brother Mohammad as my new representative at The Oasis and then we shall wait," said Saqr. "Soon, with the help of the Bani Ka'ab we shall be rid of the young Zayed and the sons of Sultan shall be at war with the Dhawahir Bedu and our enemies shall kill one another."

Dhiyab smiled, then bowed and left.

****

Zayed

Desert Site

Sheikh Ahmad with Zayed by his side and thirty of his tribesmen including Mahmud and Ibrahim were standing around a featureless desert landscape. Behind them, was a troop of camels. Several of the tribesmen were holding falcons on big leather sleeves on their arms, while others had their guns slung over their shoulders, keeping watch.

"Before the families of the Bani Yas became more interested in their precious Pearl trade," said Sheikh Ahmad, "your ancestors were great Bedu of the desert."

"The Pearling boats have gone," replied Zayed. "There is no more Pearl trade."

"And there is the lesson Zayed," smiled Sheikh Ahmad. "If a man does not know his past or where he comes from, then he is blind to the future and without direction. That is why your family has been in such turmoil."

Sheikh Ahmad raised his hand and the men disbursed and one by one the tribesmen mounted their camels and began to move away. Sheikh Ahmad signaled to Zayed to get on the camel next to him.

Chapter 3

"Out here, there can be no confusion without causing death. This is the desert Zayed. This is your ancestry," said the Sheikh.

Sheikh Ahmad tapped his camel and it groaned once more before it got up and shuffled away. Zayed initially struggled to get his camel up and away, until finally, it let out a belching groan and got up to follow the Sheikh.

****

Desert Hunt

Across a horizon, three men on camels, then ten, then thirty then fifty men on camels fan out across the desert landscape. Above the entourage a squadron of falcons hover and swirl for prey.

The Bedu tribesmen and Zayed stop to witness a Falcon sitting on a mortally injured deer.

"Praise be to God," yelled Sheikh Ahmad. "What a mighty victory."

"I did not even think it was possible for a falcon to do this?" asked Zayed.

Zayed

One of the tribesmen dismounted and came forward calling the name of the bird, who returned to his sleeve.

Sheikh Ahmad smiled as he dismounted from his camel followed by Zayed and the rest of the tribesmen. Sheikh Ahmad moved over to the crippled deer and unsheathed the janbiya (dagger) from his waist. He stopped and signalled for Zayed to come closer.

Zayed hesitated at first but once he is next to Sheikh Ahmad, the Sheikh handed him the dagger.

"Do not think. Do not hesitate," said the Sheikh. "Be firm and quick and honour its life and such a blessing from God."

Zayed took the dagger and stared for a moment at the deer, that is still in shock, with its laboured breath. The Sheikh pointed to a position between the ribs of the beast. Then in one firm stroke, Zayed raised the dagger and plunged it into the deer at the position he had been shown and the deer ceased breathing.

Zayed got up and walked back to Sheikh Ahmad. "Now you are a warrior," smiled the Sheikh.

Sheikh Ahmad then pointed to the dagger. "This is now yours."

Zayed lifted up the dagger, still dripping in blood as the men around them cry out and applaud.

Chapter 3

****

Desert Camp

It was night time at the Bedouin desert camp and a large fire illuminated a string of tents, with laughter and animated conversation. The women were camped to one side and the men in an adjoining circle. Other tribesmen stood in the shadows guarding the camp with their guns.

Just away from the full brightness of the fire, but within the sight of the guards was Sheikh Ahmad and Zayed wearing his dagger at the front of his robes.

"Zayed look to the night sky, what do you see?" asked the Sheikh.

"Thousands and thousands of stars," replied Zayed.

"Yes but you see more," smiled the Sheikh. "You see the hand of creation of the God of all the universe who is watching over us."

"I do not understand what you mean," said Zayed.

"Zayed, one day you will learn that being the father and teacher of a tribe is a heavy responsibility. A man with any conscience cannot but be affected by what he must do to preserve the balance and order."

Zayed

A voice called out and the music and animated conversation stopped. A tribesman came over to Sheikh Ahmad and Zayed.

"They are waiting," the tribesman said.

Sheikh Ahmad nodded before turning back to Zayed.

"Come," said Sheikh Ahmad. "Now you shall see the most difficult part of being a Sheikh."

Zayed followed the Sheikh to a main tent. Inside, the tent was full of people sitting around. Tribesmen with guns were guarding the entrance as Sheikh Ahmad accompanied by Zayed entered the tent. Sheikh Ahmad signalled for Zayed to sit to the side next to Mahmud, so he has an uninterrupted view.

Once he had sat down, the Sheikh signalled and a tribesman at the entrance of tent yelled out.

"The people of the first matter come now forward."

From the entrance of the tent, an old bedu man came forward and prostrated himself before the Sheikh.

Zayed looked over at Mahmud. "What is going on?" he whispered to Mahmud.

Mahmud looked at the young Zayed. "Every night we put up camp, then the local Bedu of the area come to see the Sheikh to call for justice," said Mahmud quietly.

The old Bedu Man continues to plead and speak with the Sheikh, as Zayed looked to Mahmud again.

"What if they have done something wrong?" said Zayed to Mahmud.

"Then often it will be a fine," said Mahmud as the Sheikh raised his hand. "But if it is serious-"

"Silence!" a loud voice at the entrance of the tent yelled and there was utter silence in the tent.

"I see nothing wrong with this man," said Sheikh Ahmad. "The goat was loose and he saw it as a wild goat. He needed it for his family to survive and he has brought a good goat here to replace the one taken."

The Sheikh signalled for the Old Bedu Man to get up. "You are free to go," smiled the Sheikh.

The Old Bedu Man got up and continued to bow as he retreated from the tent. The mumbling and talking amongst people within the tent resumed.

"The people of the second matter come now forward," yelled a loud voice at the entrance to the tent.

There was shouting and crying from the back of the tent as two men came forward. The women continued to wail and moan at the back of the tent.

"Silence!" yelled the booming voice of a tribesman.

Zayed

The tent goes deathly quiet again.

"Bring forward the brother," called the announcer.

A scrawny looking young man, only a few years older than Zayed is brought forward by two tribesmen and dropped in front of the Sheikh.

"Your brother is accused of killing one of your cousins," said Sheikh Ahmad. "Yet he has run away rather than face his punishment. Now it has fallen to me to restore justice and stop a blood feud between your family and your cousins. Do you understand?"

The young man nodded his head hesitatingly, without looking up.

"You are the next eldest after your brother who is a coward and your mother is blessed with two more younger sons," added the Sheikh. "Thus I must rule."

Sheikh Ahmad looked down before looking back at the accused son in front of him.

"May God be my witness that justice of his laws must be done to preserve peace amongst the tribes," said the Sheikh.

Instantly, the women in the back of the tent erupt and there is screaming and crying.

"Take him away," commanded the Sheikh.

Chapter 3

Sheikh Ahmad signalled, then stood up and exited to the back of the tent as the young man, still protesting his innocence was dragged from the tent.

"Come Zayed," said Mahmud, following the Sheikh and others emptying the tent.

Mahmud took Zayed to the exit of the tent. Outside, the tribesmen had formed a circle keeping the women and children at bay. Mahmud took Zayed around to the side of the circle of men so he could look more closely.

"But this man did not commit the crime?" asked Zayed.

"Yet you heard what the Sheikh said," replied Mahmud.

The largest and tallest of the tribesmen came forward with a large sword towards the circle of men. They immediately stepped out of the way to let him through before closing ranks.

"If there is no honour, there is no law," added Mahmud. "And if there is no law, then our people are finished."

The great sword was lifted and thrust back down, making a dull thud sound, followed by the collective gasp of everyone as witnesses.

Zayed, rubbed his eyes as he looked over and saw Sheikh Ahmad near the edge of the tent doing the same. Then Sheikh Ahmad turned away so no one could see his emotions.

Chapter 4

The Desert

Sheikh Ahmad and Zayed walked from the tents to the top of a large sand dune next to the camp. Sheikh Ahmad signalled for Zayed to get down on the ground to watch. In front of them over the other side of the sand ridge was a tribesman finishing digging a hole. The sun glinting on pieces of metal in a 'L'shape for a hundred yards around the hole.

"A man who hunts in the forest puts his faith in a loyal dog," said the Sheikh. "Yet a man of the desert must learn to trust his falcon."

Sheikh Ahmad pointed to the Bedu tribesman as the man checked a net connected to the "L" shape of rings and string. "The falcon is a cautious bird. It does not give its trust easily," added the Sheikh. "The catcher must be careful that the trap will not injure the bird."

The Bedu tribesman then walked over to a small cage and tied a string around the leg of a pigeon, flapping its wings. He tied the pigeon to a wooden perch and then returned to the hole and covered himself.

"Now we wait," said the Sheikh.

The pigeon kept flapping and soon after a falcon came down and struck the pigeon. In that instant the tribesman released the net from the hoops and both the pigeon and falcon were caught together.

"There you are!" yelled the Sheikh.

They watched as the catcher pinned down the falcon and then tied up its talons before putting a leather hood over its eyes.

"Now he must immediately name the bird and begin training," said the Sheikh.

"Why is the name so important?" asked Zayed.

"Every bird in the camp must have a different name," replied the Sheikh. "The bird must become accustomed to the sound of the voice of the falconer and to their name. When they hear their name they know it is time to come home."

****

Zayed observed the training of the falcon by the tribesman over time as Sheikh Ahmad spoke.

"The falconer must be constantly with the falcon for the first few weeks to establish as close a bond as possible. During these days, the falconer

holds the bird on his sleeve while familiarizing it to the lure."

The falconer holding the falcon on his sleeve and holding the lure.

"By night the tethers on the talons are connected to a short cord to a small perch so the bird has some freedom of movement, with the falconer always calling its name."

An assistant to the falconer removed the hood from the bird, enabling it to see and to make short flights to the location of the falconer and the lure with some raw meat.

"After a few weeks, the falconer lets the bird travel short distances to the lure to be rewarded with some meat."

An unlucky pigeon was tethered on a pole. In the distance the falconer released his bird. Within moments, the falcon swooped and took the pigeon in its talons and flew back to the falconer.

"Then the bird is trained with live prey and taught not to kill it, so that it may be justly despatched in accord with the will of God. For not even a humble pigeon may suffer, even in the teaching of such a noble companion as a falcon."

****

Al Muwaiji Fort

Salmah, Shakhbut, Hazza and Khaled arrived on horses to a fortress (Al Muaiji Fort).

"Do nothing unless you have to," said Salmah. "We need your uncle Mohammad to be an ally."

Shakhbut nodded as they get off their horses and hand them to attendants in the courtyard.

Inside the main hall was Mohammad bin Zayed and several guards including Dhiyab bin Saqr, leaning against the wall.

"Welcome sons of Sultan, said Mohammad. "Welcome Sheikha Salmah. May God grant you many blessings."

"Excuse me Dhiyab if I do not extend the same courtesy to you," replied Salmah coldly.

"If you intend to break the terms of us coming here in peace," said Shakhbut, "then I assure you our men will ensure none leave this fort standing -"

Dhiyab laughed. "No one wishes to break the truce of your visit Shakhbut or to bring harm to the sons of Sultan and his widow," he said.

Chapter 4

"It is why I called you and why Dhiyab is here," said Mohammad. "To discuss terms of peace."

"Peace. Terms," yelled Shakhbut. "His father murdered my father the head of this family -"

"And your father murdered his brother Hamad," interrupted Dhiyab. "So how much more blood needs to be spilt Shakhbut before this feud is over?"

"Just a little more -"

"Enough!" yelled Mohammad interrupting Shakhbut. "I am the head of the family for the Oasis and I alone speak for the Al Bu Falah tribe here. No one shall bring harm or dishonour to one another while I am the representative of the Eastern Region."

"What is it then that you bring as a peace offering Dhiyab?" asked Salmah.

Dhiyab smiled. "My father recognises your claim to Al Jahili and shall not move against you Sheikha or your sons, in exchange for your solemn submission before witnesses here not to bear arms against him."

Shakhbut laughed. "This is nothing! Empty words from the son of -"

Salmah put her hand up, cutting Shakhbut off. Salmah bowed to Dhiyab. "Please tell your father that we are grateful for his wish to see no more blood be spilled," she said. "But as you can see young Dhiyab, the wounds of my children remain raw. I assure you I seek only peace for my sons and our family and good health for your father."

Dhiyab bowed to Salmah. "Very well Sheikha," he said. "I shall pass on to my father your best intentions and we shall meet again soon."

****

Sheikh Ahmad and several tribesmen were lying on a desert dune watching young Zayed prepare a falcon trap below, finishing the preparation of the pigeon and then getting into his hole.

Soon after a male peregrine falcon struck at the pigeon and Zayed pulled the string and the netting flies over and misses the pigeon as the young male falcon flies away. The tribesmen start laughing as Sheikh Ahmad shook his head.

"Patience Zayed," smiled Sheikh Ahmad. "Prepare the trap again."

As the sun is setting, Zayed becomes sleepy in his hole when suddenly a great female peregrine falcon struck at the pigeon. Zayed was startled at first and then starts pulling on the rope and the net springs over trapping the pigeon and the female falcon.

Chapter 4

"She is a huge falcon Zayed," yelled the Sheikh. "Quick, grab her and settle her down so she does not break a wing."

The tribesmen applaud Zayed as he wraps the legs of the falcon and puts the leather hood over the head of the bird.

****

Zayed was standing proudly holding his huge female peregrine falcon. Her feet tethered and a leather cap on her head.

"What have you named her?" asked Mahmud.

"Azima," said Zayed proudly. "As she is magnificent and grand."

Sheikh Ahmad nodded his head. "A good name," he smiled.

****

Zayed continued to train his falcon with the guidance of Sheikh Ahmad, as the Sheikh spoke.

"*Remember Zayed, the falconer and the falcon must become one spirit.*"

Zayed held Azima the falcon on his sleeve and holding the lure.

"*Use her name. Call her. Be deliberate and clear.*"

Mahmud held Azima the falcon with Zayed in the distance holding the lure and some raw meat. Mahmud removed the leather hood and the restraint and Azima the falcon flies to Zayed. There was absolute joy on the face of Zayed.

"*And if you have listened and learned everything you have been shown then maybe after some weeks, you will be ready Zayed to take your falcon on a hunt.*"

A tethered pigeon on a pole. In the distance Zayed with Azima the falcon. He released her and she snatches the pigeon and returned it to him.

Zayed was sitting proudly on his camel, as Azima the falcon sat on his sleeve as he surveyed the desert in front of him and around him.

Chapter 5

Al Jahili Fort, Compound

Mohammad bin Sultan and his men rushed into the compound of Al Jahili Fort.

Mohammad, looking especially nervous, waved his hand, before jumping from his horse. "Get everyone out quickly," he commanded. "We do not have much time."

He followed his men into the main buildings of the fort.

Inside, people were already running from room to room, grabbing items. As Mohammad entered the main hall, he saw Salmah and Shakhbut were arguing with one of his men.

"Salmah we have to hurry," yelled Mohammad. "Saqr has sent his sons and men to kill you. I have to hide you quickly or else he will suspect me as well."

Shakhbut stopped arguing with his mother and turned to Mohammad. "If he has committed all his men," replied Shakhbut, "then this is the moment we have been waiting for to strike."

Salmah grabbed the arm of Shakhbut. "No. I will not have you or your brothers throw away your lives," she yelled. "Saqr is far too dangerous."

Mohammad nodded his head in agreement. "Your mother is right Shakhbut. Now is not the time."

Shakhbut broke from the grip of his mother. "All Saqr has is fear," he said. "And I will not live another day under it. If God wills this be my last day, then so be it."

Shakhbut followed by Khaled stormed out of the hall. Salmah made one last attempt to stop him, but her reach was obstructed by Mohammad Bin Zayed.

"He is old enough Salmah," said Mohammad. "We have no time left. I must get you and the women and children to safety."

Salmah dropped to her knees and started crying.

****

Zayed was standing with Azima his falcon on his sleeve with Sheikh Ahmad by his side.

"It is time Zayed to let Azima continue on her journey," said the Sheikh.

"Why? It has been such a short time. Why cannot she stay?" protested Zayed.

"We can own nothing in this life," replied the Sheikh. "All we can be are good custodians. If you keep her over summer, then she may get sick from the humidity and heat and die."

Zayed huffed and released the tethers of Azima, before removing her leather hood.

"Go! You are free," said Zayed to Azima.

For a moment the falcon did not move, until Zayed shifted his arm and then she took flight.

"She understands it is time," said the Sheikh, patting Zayed on the shoulder. "If it be the will of God, then come next winter she will find you."

Zayed and Sheikh Ahmad watched as the falcon flew two circles, before she flew away into the distance. Zayed dropped his head, when he could no longer see the bird. Yet the Sheikh remained fixed looking forward.

On the horizon was the sight of a lone rider on a horse approaching camp. As the lone rider finally reached the outskirts of the camp, the tribesmen intercepted him and brought him to the Sheikh. After the tribesman spoke briefly to the rider, they signalled for the Sheikh to come over.

"Excuse me Zayed," said the Sheikh. "I will be a moment."

Zayed

Sheikh Ahmad stepped across to the rider who appeared agitated, before the rider spoke into the ear of the Sheikh. The Sheikh then looked over at Zayed before whispering something briefly back to the rider who bowed and then departed.

Sheikh Ahmad returned to Zayed. "I must return at once to the Oasis. You will stay with the men here and will be safe."

"What has happened?" asked Zayed.

"I shall call for you once I return," smiled the Sheikh. "Till then you will be safe here. Stay with the men."

Zayed nodded as he watched the Sheikh and most of his men disappear into the distance, leaving only Mahmud and five other tribesmen at the camp.

****

Zayed and Mahmud and the remaining tribesmen moved along the sand dunes, until Mahmud signalled to stop. Zayed keeps looking back at three of the Bedu tribesmen at the end of the line who kept staring at him.

"I don't like them Mahmud," whispered Zayed to Mahmud.

Chapter 5

Mahmud laughed. "I wouldn't smile at you if you kept staring at me either Zayed," chucked Mahmud.

Mahmud pointed to some shrub bushes at the bottom of a sand ridge. "We will camp here for the night," said Mahmud.

Zayed and the men dismount and prepared the camp.

****

Mahmud and Zayed were sitting down around a camp fire with two of the other tribesmen.

"Why did the Sheikh not tell me what has happened?" asked Zayed.

"He has his reasons," said Mahmud.

"I would not have cried if he told me they were dead. I was brave when I saw my father killed."

"There is nothing wrong if a man cries," smiled Mahmud, "nor if he shows fear Zayed. Only that he chooses to do the right thing when the time comes. Maybe he does not know if it is safe so he -"

Mahmud suddenly stopped smiling and speaking as a sword had been thrust through his back and out the front of his chest. At the same moment, other two tribesmen at the camp fire were also slain, before they could reach for their guns. Mahmud turned his head to Zayed still sitting in shock.

"Ka'ab assassins," coughed Mahmud. "Run, Zayed. Run."

Zayed at first was frozen in fear, as Mahmud took his last gasp. Zayed locked eyes on the Ka'ab tribesmen who had just murdered Mahmud.

But before the Ka'ab tribesmen even moved, Zayed jumped back behind one of the tents and started running full speed into the darkness of the desert.

Chapter 6

Desert

Zayed kept running and running until he stopped and looked briefly at the sight of the tents and the fire far away. He hid for a moment behind some scrub bushes that had taken hold on a sand ridge.

He looked back at his tracks in the moon light and could see that his tracks gave away his position. He grabbed one of the branches of a bush and using his dagger cut it off the tree. Zayed then walked backwards down the slope, away from the ridge and wiped clear each of his foot prints.

He stopped and then started walking backwards in parallel to the ridge until he met up with his old tracks, then started wiping away his tracks toward the ridge.

On top of the ridge, behind the bush, he dug a hole near its base, using some sticks and debris to help stabilise the sand and dirt. He then made a cover for the hole and got inside.

****

As the morning light pierced through the small imperfections in the cover of his hiding hole, Zayed heard the sound and speech of some men nearby. The men came closer but then stopped. Staying deathly still, Zayed could hear them move off.

****

It was night time and Zayed finally crawled out of the hole and stretched his limbs to recover from the cramped conditions. He looked around to see no one, no camp fires, no sign of life. He was all alone.

He looked to the sky to get his bearings and began to move north-west and toward the Oasis.

****

Al Jahili Fort, Compound

Dhiyab bin Saqr and Rashid bin Saqr with their men rode into the compound of Al Jahili Fort.

"Find them," growled Dhiyab.

The men dismounted and fanned out across the fort, while Dhiyab and Rashid remained on horseback.

Chapter 6

There were the sounds of smashing and crashing before a tribesman returned to him and bowed.

"No one is here," said the tribesman.

"Then burn it down," replied Dhiyab.

The tribesman nodded and the men of Dhiyab and Rashid began to torch the supplies around the fort and the woodwork.

****

Al Hosn Fort, Main Hall

Saqr was sitting in the main hall, drinking coffee with his brother Khalifa and several other men, when he heard some shouting from outside.

"Dhiyab is that you?" said Saqr excitedly. "Rashid come here and tell me of the news?"

At that moment Shakhbut appeared with Khaled and several of the Dhawahir Bedu tribesmen. The face of Saqr was first one of horror, then quickly defiance.

"Sorry to disappoint you uncle," grinned Shakhbut.

"I am head of the Al Bu Falah," said Saqr defiantly. "You are bound by law to respect me."

"The family and position of Sheikh, yes. You, no," said Shakhbut.

Zayed

Shakhbut pulled out his sword as Khalifa bin Zayed stood up and stepped in front of Saqr, shielding him.

"Shakhbut too much blood has already been shed in this family," said Khalifa. "Put your sword down and let us resolve this peacefully."

"Peacefully Uncle? Saqr has already tried to kill us recently and again tonight."

"Your too late," laughed Saqr. "Killing me won't bring back Zayed."

Khalifa swung around and stared at Saqr.

"What have you done this time?"

Khalifa stepped out of the way and as Saqr stepped back, he tripped on his robes and fell to the floor.

"The war has already started between the Ka'ab and the Dhawahir and only I can stop it," grinned Saqr.

Khalifa glanced at Shakhbut and both men looked back at Saqr.

****

Zayed Lost In Desert

Zayed was lost in the desert. He came to a gap in the dunes and some stony ground. One by one, Zayed picked up a number of large stones and then brought them together. One by one, he dug them into the dirt, remembering the words of Sheikh Ahmad.

"If you can find no water, then find some good sized stones and bury them halfway, then just before the sun rises turn them over and you shall find some moisture."

Zayed turned over the stones and licked away the dew on each of them before continuing on his journey.

"The sun rises from the east and sets in the west. The sand forms at 90 degrees to the wind. So if the wind is from the east the sand will shape north to south. If the dunes are horned then the point will be away from the prevailing wind."

Zayed continued to walk slowly across a gravelly plain, looking weaker and weaker.

"Above all else my son you must find water or else you shall surely die in the desert. Look for flies and especially mosquitoes as they are your friends and tell you that you are near to water."

Zayed collapsed from exhaustion in front of a short bush with two desert flowers on it. Suddenly he opened one eye and spotted a bee landing on one of the flowers.

Zayed

"But if you find a bee my son you are saved. As a bee will fly in a straight line to and from water up to 800 yards."

As the bee left the bush, Zayed followed it over several dunes until finally he spotted a moist spot between the dunes surrounded by some bushes and greenery. He scrambled down and started digging into the sand, until water formed into a shallow pool. As the sun began to set, Zayed prostrated himself in prayer next to the pool of water.

"Do not neglect your prayers. Even in hunger or sickness or thirst. For this is when our calls to heaven hold greater meaning."

In the morning, Zayed awoke to find a hare drinking at the pool of water. But just as Zayed lunged over to try and catch it, he missed and the hare hopped away.

Zayed passed out again to be woken by a thud on his head. He slowly opened his eyes and felt his head, then looked at his hand. It was covered in blood. He got up to see it is not his blood but the blood of the hare. Next to him proudly guarding the prize is Azima his falcon.

"Azima you came back!"

Chapter 6

The bird stepped away for a moment, unsure as to this excitement and his sudden movements. Zayed calmed himself down.

"It is OK Azima. I am fine. Thank you."

Zayed smiled. "Good bird."

Zayed

Chapter 7

Al Hosn Fort

Inside the main hall was Shakhbut, with his brothers Hazza and Khaled and their uncles Khalifa Bin Zayed and Mohammad Bin Zayed. Meanwhile, Salmah sat impatiently with the women behind the screen.

Also in the hall were Sheikh Saeed bin Maktoum of Dubai, Sheikh Sultan Bin Saqr Al Qasimi and Sheikh Rashid Bin Humaid Al Nuami.

Khalifa stood up to address the meeting. "I have called you all here because the Al Bu Falah seek only peace," he said. "Yet Saqr and his sons sought only war. We have no quarrel with the Bani Yas."

"Why did you not accept being the head of the Al Bu Falah?" asked Sheikh Saeed bin Maktoum. "My family respects you Khalifa. The Al Bu Falasah of Dubai only want peace and unity between the Bani Yas."

"As do the Al Qawasim of Sharjah," said Sheikh Sultan Bin Saqr Al Qasimi.

"And the Al Nu'aim of Ajman," added Sheikh Rashid Bin Humaid Al Nuami

"But Saqr was my blood through the marriage of my son," said Sheikh Saeed, "and so Shakhbut must atone for his actions."

"Shakhbut did not kill Saqr," said Khalifa. "I did."

A collective gasp enveloped the room.

As Khalifa continued to speak, the final moments of the life of Saqr become clearer. It was true that Shakhbut was holding Saqr by the throat in the same room. But it was also true that Khalifa pushed Shakhbut aside and took the sword himself.

"As the eldest son of the Al Bu Falah, I told Shakhbut to step aside for it was my duty to hold Saqr to account for the murder of my brother Sultan," recounted Khalifa.

In the final moments of the life of Saqr, it was Shakhbut who stepped aside when Saqr rose to his feet, only to be seized by two of the men of Khalifa, who forced Saqr back onto his knees.

"Too much blood has been shed. The law needed to be restored, so I am responsible."

Khalifa raised the sword above Saqr and the final moments of the life of Saqr ended.

"Then the Al Bu Falasah of Dubai have no quarrel with Shakhbut," said Sheikh Saeed, "as what was done was lawful and we respect your claim as Sheikh."

"Not I, it is Shakhbut who shall be head of the Al Bu Falah," said Khalifa. "And the sons of Saqr must atone for the killings at the oasis and the murder of my youngest nephew Zayed."

Shakhbut signalled for the sons of Saqr to be brought forward.

Into the room were brought the bound and bloodied figures of Dhiyab bin Saqr and Rashid bin Saqr. They were then forced to kneel in front of the assembled meeting.

****

Outside, in the distance, a lone young figure on a camel with a falcon, followed by three then ten then thirty more camel riders approached Abu Dubai and Al Hosn Fort. It was Zayed followed by Sheikh Ahmad and his tribesmen as they move through the streets toward the Al Hosn Fort.

****

Inside the fort, the fate of the sons of Saqr continued.

"Sheikh Shakhbut what you choose to do concerning the judgement of Abu Dhabi is your domain," said Sheikh Saeed. "For the sake of my daughter in law and my son I only ask for wisdom and compassion to end the bloodshed."

"The law is very clear Sheikh Saeed," replied Shakhbut. "An eye for an eye, is it not? Then all I ask is for justice for my dead brother. Nothing more or less."

A commotion erupted at the back of the hall, as Shakhbut and the other leaders looked to the entrance. Into the main hall raced Samir and brushed past to stop in front of Shakhbut.

"It is the Bedu," exclaimed Samir excitedly. "It is Sheikh Ahmad. Zayed is alive!"

There was a collective roar as everyone looked at each other, including Dhiyab and Rashid. Then into the hall stepped Sheikh Ahmad and Zayed, carrying Azima his falcon.

Salmah could not contain herself and she broke past the grail and embraced Zayed, who handed the falcon to one of the tribesmen.

"My son," cried Salmah, "they told me you were dead."

"God has something planned for your son Sheikha Salmah," said Sheikh Ahmad. "My men have witnessed it themselves. He was saved from the desert by an angel in the form of that great falcon."

Chapter 7

Salmah continued to kiss and hug Zayed until he broke from the embrace. "Mother-".

Salmah then signalled to her sons.

"Shakhbut, Hazza, Khaled and Zayed come here," she yelled.

"Woman, I am now the Sheikh and head of the-"

"And I am your mother," interrupted Salmah. "Come here NOW."

There was mumbling and grumbling.

"Silence!" yelled Sheikh Ahmad in a booming voice and the room went silent.

"Before all here present, I want you to promise," said Salmah. "Promise before heaven, before God that you shall protect one another and not harm one another; that you will forgive others of the Al Bu Falah and end this madness of an eye for an eye."

"But mother," protested Shakhbut, "the law says that Dhiyab and Rashid must be puni-"

"The law says forgive," interrupted Salmah. "The law says honour and give praise for all that is given to us by God. Your brother is alive Shakhbut. Promise with your brothers and give us in trust a true kingdom of conscience."

Shakhbut scanned the faces of everyone in the room witnessing the scene and back to his brothers and his mother and nodded his head.

"I promise," mumbled Shakhbut

"Louder," demanded Salmah.

"I promise by almighty God, that I shall never use force against any member of the Al Bu Falah or the Bani Yas and that I shall protect my brothers and our tribe, said Shakhbut.

"I promise," said Hazza.

"I promise," said Khaled.

"I so promise," said Zayed.

"Then so be it," smiled Salmah. "I promise I shall return to my place a happy woman knowing the curse has ended."

All the Sheikhs bowed as Salmah rejoined the other women behind the grail.

"God wills it to be a time of miracles," said Sheikh Saeed.

"Dhiyab and Rashid and the rest of the family of Saqr shall be spared," said Shakhbut. "But shall be exiled to Bahrain. Nor shall they be permitted to return without permission and only for a day, leaving before sun down. Nor shall they be permitted to marry into any of the other families of the Al Bu Falah. This is my ruling."

Shakhbut then got up and stepped across to Zayed and embraced him.

"It is time for you to return to Abu Dhabi little brother," smiled Shakhbut.

Zayed looked over at Sheikh Ahmad and back to Shakhbut. "But the Oasis is my home with the Bedu," he frowned.

Chuckles from the Sheikhs watching.

"Do not dishonour me before the Bani Yas Zayed. I will ask you one more time to return or else you too shall be banished-"

Salmah jumped back from behind the grail as Shakhbut raised his hand to her.

"You promised mother, as I have also pledged," said Shakhbut

Shakhbut zeroed his focus on Zayed. "What shall your decision be?"

Zayed looked back at his mother and then at Sheikh Ahmad before he turned his back on his brother and walked toward the entrance. All in the room except Shakhbut begin smiling.

"Very well," yelled Shakhbut. "You can remain at the Oasis but you will be banished from Abu Dhabi."

Zayed

Sheikh Ahmad bowed as did the other Bedu and they turned and left.

"Go and be a goat herder Zayed," called out Shakhbut. "But don't come back and plead for forgiveness."

Chapter 8

Abu Dhabi, 1936

The village of Abu Dhabi looked even poorer than it did ten years earlier. A freighter was docked at the solitary jetty, off-loading military vehicles. In the distance the shadow of a British Navy frigate.

Half a dozen British soldiers and three men in civilian "safari" clothing (Stephen Longrigg, John Howes and Patrick Stobart) were standing on the jetty watching as a third vehicle was being off-loaded from the freighter. Stephen Longrigg looked over at John Howes.

"About this Sheikh Zakhbut fellow again?" asked Stephen Longrigg.

"Sheikh Shakhbut," replied John Howes. "Very difficult fellow. Seems to be stuck in the 19th Century. Suspicious of everyone. A bit like an Elizabethan tragedy. The Al Bu Falah just can't stop killing one another."

A British captain (Captain Mallory) stepped up to the three men, but did not interrupt the conversation.

"Ah that is not entirely accurate sir," added Patrick Stobart. "The mother made the Sheikh and all his brothers swear a holy oath to end the blood feud in front of the Bani Yas-"

"The what?" interrupted Stephen Longrigg.

"The federation of tribes controlling most of the Trucial States sir," said John Howes.

The final British soldiers stepped into the vehicles behind the men in conversation.

"There hasn't been any assassinations for at least eight years," said Patrick Stobart.

Stephen Longrigg looked over at Captain Mallory and acknowledged his presence.

"That's a comfort," smiled Stephen Longrigg. "In any event, I trust we have enough men and firepower for any eventuality?"

Captain Mallory nodded affirmatively. "We are ready sir," he said.

When Stephen Longrigg gave Captain Mallory the signal, the captain raised his hand and the three vehicles started their motors.

"Better to be prepared," smiled Stephen Longrigg.

The men followed Captain Mallory to the lead vehicle and got in. The three vehicles leave the jetty watched on by curious locals.

****

Chapter 8

Al Hosn Fort, Main Hall

Samir dressed in tribal robes ran up to Sheikh Shakhbut sitting in the main hall and bowed. "The British are here," he said.

Shakhbut acknowledged him. "Let them wait a few minutes," he said. "Get me my glasses and papers."

Samir departed as another attendant handed the Sheikh a set of reading glasses and assortment of papers.

In the courtyard of the fort, Stephen Longrigg, John Howes (holding a brief case), along with Patrick Stobart, Captain Mallory and several British soldiers remain impatiently waiting. Around them, the tribesmen look on with suspicion.

Samir stepped out into the courtyard and smiled to the party. "His Highness Sheikh Shakhbut bin Zayed Al Nahyan shall see you in a moment," he said. "Please wait here."

After Samir had left, John Howes looked over at Patrick Stobart.

"Damn rude if you ask me, all this waiting around," he mumbled.

"It is their country," replied Patrick Stobart.

"Right. So I am not going to suffer the same indignity of the weeks of grovelling I did with the Saudis, only to be trumped by the damn Americans," added Stephen Longrigg. "If this Sheikh wants shiny bars of gold, then that is what he is going to get for his agreement."

Samir returned.

"The Sheikh shall see you now," said Samir. "Please follow me."

The men follow Samir into the main hall.

The British party entered the main hall as the Tribal guards straightened up and stare at the British soldiers. Sheikh Shakhbut remained transfixed on reading pieces of paper with his glasses. He did not even look up until he handed the papers and glasses to Samir.

"Bring this back to me as soon as we are finished," said Shakhbut to Samir. "I am very busy."

Samir hesitated at first and then bowed, before disappearing. Finally, Shakhbut turned and looked at the British standing patiently in front of him. Stephen Longrigg stepped forward.

"Your Highness, my name is Stephen Hemsley Longrigg and I represent the Iraq Petroleum Company and the British Crown. I am here because we have formed a new company called the Petroleum Development Trucial Coast Ltd and we would like your permission to explore for oil within your lands."

Shakhbut rubbed his face, looking away, then stared back at Longrigg.

"I am aware of the Americans and their agreement with the Al Saud. Yet our people are fiercely protective of what is rightfully theirs."

Longrigg let a wry smile creep onto his face as he turned to John Howes. Howes then opened up a brief case as the tribal guards around the room start twitching. Howes hesitated for a moment, then continued to open it.

Inside was a large bar of pure gold. He handed it to Longrigg. The eyes of several guards and attendants bulged open at the site of the brick of gold while Shakhbut appeared little impressed at first.

"Let me get to the point then Sheikh," said Stephen Longrigg. "100,000 Indian rupees per year during this exploration phase, then 200,000 rupees yearly once oil is found in good quantities and an additional three rupees on every tonne exported for the next 75 years. Or to put it another way, you can have this gold bar today if we have a deal, then two more each month while we explore then a whole lot of gold bars when we find oil."

Longrigg reached over and handed the gold bar to Shakhbut who appeared disinterested in it, as he held it, then turned it around, watching as it caught the light coming into the room.

"Of course we will need your best interpreter and someone who knows the tribes and the lands well," added Stephen Longrigg.

Shakhbut nodded again without looking up, as he continued to study the gold bar. Longrigg looked over to Patrick Stobart who gave him a wry smile back.

"So do we have an agreement Your Highness?" asked Stephen Longrigg expectantly. "Your Highness?"

Finally Shakhbut looked up as his face hardened. He thrust the bar back at Longrigg who stepped back at first to avoid collecting it from him.

"Is there nothing you do not think you can purchase British?" growled Shakhbut.

Longrigg appeared shocked and waved his hands.

"No it is a gift Your Highness. It is yours to keep. My deepest apologies if you felt that-"

Shakhbut withdrew his arm and returned to studying the gold bar.

Chapter 8

"The Bedu are not easily swayed. But our people need work," said Shakhbut.

"Then we shall come to that when we go to see them," replied Stephen Longrigg. "I am sure you can provide them some compensation as well from all the gold Your Highness?"

Shakhbut nodded.

"If God wills it, then let it be."

Longrigg extended his hand and the Sheikh finally acknowledged him and shook hands.

"Excellent," replied Stephen Longrigg before signalling for Howes and Stobart to come forward. "Howes and Stobart here will prepare the paper work, in English and Arabic of course. Now where do we find this interpreter and guide you have promised?"

Zayed

Chapter 9

Al Muwaiji Fort, The Oasis, 1936

A young girl Hassa came running out from the main entrance of the fort.

"Zayed! Zayed, where are you?"

She ran around the corner, past some camels sitting down, and across to a group of tribesmen. They stopped talking when they see her. Hassa touched the shoulder of one tribesman with his back to her and he turned and smiled. It was not Zayed.

Instead, the tribesman pointed to a solitary figure in traditional robes standing on a higher ridge beyond the fort, as a great falcon return to his arm.

"Zayed!" the girl shouted.

He turned around toward the direction of the calling, to reveal himself to be a tall and handsome young man, flashing perfect teeth and a smile. It is Zayed.

The young girl dragged Zayed into the compound as the guards watched on.

"Hassa, you'll dislocate my arm if you pull any harder."

"Father wants to see you urgently."

"What if I don't want to see your father?"

"Then the father of Hassa will have to come and seek you out," said a voice from behind him. Zayed swung around to see Mohammad bin Khalifa. He bowed to Zayed as Hassa suddenly composed herself, bowed to her father and then ran away, glancing briefly back at Zayed.

"She is wilful," smiled Zayed.

"And I am sure she likes you as well Zayed," grinned Mohammad. "Cousin. Your brother Sheikh Shakhbut has sent word he has asked you to help some British that are coming."

Zayed started laughing and shaking his head as Mohammad frowned.

"What is so funny?"

"Shakhbut banished me from Abu Dhabi," replied Zayed. "He would never ask for my help unless it was to open the door to King Solomon's Mine."

Mohammad allowed himself a brief smile.

"I knew it!" added Zayed. "So then the rumours are true. The British have come to try and take our land."

"Our oil, not our land," said Mohammad. "Zayed you are the best of all the Al BuFalah at English and Shakhbut knows it. He has lifted the banishment and is in need of your help."

Chapter 9

"Why then should I help a European power continue to keep us under their foot?" protested Zayed.

"Because if you don't then I am sure Shakhbut will find someone among the Bani Yas who cares far less about the people than you."

****

Desert Exploration

A convoy of trucks and cars snaked its way across gravel and drifting sand toward a lone horseman (Zayed), astride a sand ridge overlooking the landscape like some Arabian painting. The trucks and cars stopped. The British soldiers, civilians and then Stephen Longrigg, John Howes, Patrick Stobart and Captain Mallory step out of their vehicles and move toward Zayed on his horse. Zayed points to the valley in front of them.

"This is the spot you asked to see."

John Howes opened up a large map and folded it out on top of the dirt, so all can see. Zayed jumped off his horse and stepped over to view the map as well.

"But it is not on the map."

Zayed shook his head negatively.

"Then your map is wrong."

"This is a map by the best British Royal Surveyors," added Stephen Longrigg.

"Then the best British Royal Surveyors are wrong," replied Zayed.

"Look here -" protested Stephen Longrigg, before Patrick Stobart put up his hand to interrupt him.

"What we are just saying is that we have no record of it," said Patrick Stobart. "That's all."

"I fully understand and all I am saying is that even the smartest men make mistakes," smiled Zayed.

Zayed then reached over and picked up a pen and marked the map with the location and name of the valley.

"There! Now fixed."

Stephen Longrigg grinned.

"Where to now?"

"We need to cross the valley, but your vehicles will not make it," said Zayed.

"We have plenty of fuel and supplies," replied John Howes.

Zayed shrugged his shoulders and then stepped away.

With Zayed leading the way on horseback the men returned to their vehicles and started to follow. A few

Chapter 9

yards along, the first vehicle stopped due to having its tyres punctured and axle severed by the sharp rocks. A few moments later, the second vehicle was damaged and also stopped. The convoy ground to a halt.

"We shall camp here," smiled Zayed.

****

Desert Camp

It was dusk. Zayed, Stephen Longrigg, John Howes and Patrick Stobart were seated around a large camp fire. In the distance, the British soldiers continue to work to fix the vehicles.

"So how do you exist out here in such conditions?" asked Patrick Stobart.

"I could ask the same thing of you and all who live in such cities of concrete and stone without a soul."

Stephen Longrigg laughed.

"Well said. And it may very well be the only place untouched when war comes to the world soon."

"War?" asked Zayed.

"Hitler, Mussolini and Stalin and the Nazis," said Stephen Longrigg.

Zayed shook his head.

"Nazi Germany in Europe," said John Howes. "Surely you have heard of -"

"Yes, Europe and Germany," interrupted Zayed. "I have heard of Europe and Germany, but without books or radio or newspapers I am not familiar with such events. Maybe you could help me become more familiar?"

"I have an old set of Encyclopedia Britannica which I will see is shipped to you," offered Patrick Stobart.

"Thank you," smiled Zayed. "And a copy of those maps you have been correcting please. Especially of the Oasis."

Patrick Stobart looked over at Stephen Longrigg who nodded affirmatively.

"No one can live in isolation sheikh," said Stephen Longrigg. "The age of machines and war is upon us and whether your people like it or not, the need for oil will mean you will have to become familiar with the world."

Zayed smiled.

"I agree."

****

Al Jimi Fort

Chapter 9

Zayed arrived on horseback at the fort and home of
Sheikh Ahmad. Inside, Zayed entered the main hall to
find Sheikh Ahmad stretched out covered in blankets
with the room full of vapours and smoke.

Zayed moved over and knelt in front of Sheikh
Ahmad.

"What is the matter?" he asked.

"It is nothing," said Sheikh Ahmad, before
coughing.

Zayed shook his head.

"Let me call for a physician."

Sheikh Ahmad pointed to the older men in the
corner, mixing more herbs and stoking incense and
smoke burners.

"I have all the physicians I need."

"I mean real doctors, western doctors."

Sheikh Ahmad started laughing, before coughing
violently.

"What? To tell me I am dying," he replied. "One day
we will have doctors telling us why we are sick, but for
the moment, the mystery of life and death remains
simple."

"But I don't want to see you die," protested Zayed.

"That makes two of us. But Zayed you can no more
stop the sands of time, than force a man to be

honourable. But why then have you come? Certainly not to discuss my health."

"Shakhbut has done a deal with the British for oil. I have shown them some of the Oasis but they want to continue to explore the edge of the empty quarter and the shoreline."

"Then why do you still look concerned?" asked Sheikh Ahmad

"I fear oil and power and money will change our people and will change Shakhbut and that we are not ready for it."

Sheikh Ahmad started a coughing fit until Zayed helped him calm down.

"Zayed, all a complete man can ever do is lead by example and honour the rule of law and the laws of heaven. The rest is beyond our control."

"You are right again," said Zayed. "I am sorry for burdening you with my doubts."

"And Zayed," smiled Sheikh Ahmad, "that is why one day you will be a great leader."

Chapter 10

Abu Dhabi, 1939

Zayed rode into Abu Dhabi on a beautiful horse. The image he cast was the epitome of a postcard of a noble Bedouin. Three other Bedu followed behind him.

He stopped briefly and surveyed a vast building site (Al Manhal Palace) of hundreds of workers, digging, paving and laying stonework. He turned his horse towards Al Hosn Fort and rode away.

Al Hosn Fort

As Zayed approached the Fort, he saw Shakhbut with several guards, observing the building site from the battlements. Shakhbut waved but Zayed ignored him and entered through the main gate.

Zayed dismounted from his horse, as Samir shuffled over waving his hand.

"You have no appointment," he protested.

Zayed brushed past him as Samir looked up at Shakhbut who ignored him and instead smiled at Zayed, motioning for him to come up to the battlements.

Zayed

"Brother! Finally you have come to see my finest work."

Samir slinked away as Zayed strode over to the steps and then up to the battlements and greeted his brother.

The guards around Shakhbut acknowledged Zayed and bowed slightly as he approached his brother.

"What are you doing?" asked Zayed, as he pointed over the battlements at the building site further away.

"I am building a new palace," smiled Shakhbut proudly.

"But what about the people? What about a hospital or a school?"

Shakhbut laughed.

"You did not need a school and look at you? Why do we need western doctors trying to sell us expensive western medicines when we have been treating ourselves for thousands of years?"

"Because we don't know everything brother. Because those doctors learn about new diseases and curing people. Because Sheikh Ahmad of the Dhawahir is dying and if we had a hospital then maybe we would could help him and help others."

Shakhbut patted Zayed on the back.

Chapter 10

"Zayed I am sorry. He has been like a second father to you. But look," said Shakhbut pointing at the building site. Workers like ants were moving all over the project.

"The people don't need education. They need jobs. There is no more pearling trade. Building this palace which I shall call Al Manhal, means the poor of Abu Dhabi have work and can eat."

"But with a fraction of what the British are giving you brother, we could improve our fresh water or teach people trades that mean better jobs for a dozen generations."

"Zayed you have always been the dreamer."

The demeanour of Shakhbut quickly changed to sombre.

"But this is reality. I am the head of the family and the reality is we need a proper palace to project our strength to the other families of the Bani Yas, or else they will come and take it all from us and Al Bu Falah will cease to exist."

Shakhbut turned his back on Zayed and resumed looking out at the building site.

"So your precious schools and hospitals will have to wait," yelled Shakhbut.

Zayed

****

Jimi Village

Zayed and his guards approached Jimi Village as
hundreds of the women, all dressed in black, were
wailing. While Zayed rode past them on his horse,
some of the women and even some of the men reach
out to him, tears in their eyes. Zayed quickly
dismounted from his horse and raced into the fort.

Inside the bedroom of Sheikh Ahmad was full of
men, including Ibrahim and several other Bedu
tribesmen, as they observed an older man finishing
wrapping the body of the Sheikh in linen ready to be
taken to burial. Zayed stared at the body of Ahmad
while it was being covered, wiping tears from his eyes.

"He died without any pain," said Ibrahim to Zayed.

"I, I did not have the chance to say goodbye,"
stuttered Zayed.

"He named me as his successor before the council
as witnesses. It is lawful."

Zayed nodded without looking at Ibrahim, still
transfixed at the body of the Sheikh now wrapped for
burial.

Chapter 10

"The men love you," added Ibrahim. "I shall expect the same loyalty as you showed Ahmad, may his soul be at peace."

Zayed looked at Ibrahim and frowned, without saying a word. A group of men picked up the body to begin the procession to burial. Ibrahim shuffled away while the body was carried out of the room. Zayed followed immediately behind.

****

The Oasis, Grave Of Sheikh Ahmad

As the sun was setting, Zayed was still standing in front of the fresh grave of Sheikh Ahmad upon a hill overlooking Jimi Village and the fort.

An old man in white robes (Sheikh Yousuf Yassin), covered by a brown cloak stepped over to the grave and began a brief prayer. He finished and then turned and smiled at Zayed, patting him on the shoulder.

"Arabia has lost one of its great sons."

Zayed noticed the gold trimming on the white robes.

"Even for Riyadh?" replied Zayed. "I thought such death would favour the Al Saud?"

Zayed

"Never confuse politics young Zayed with what unites us all in the quest for the independence of all our lands from the foreign infidels. Oil and power may soon make us enemies, yet in faith we will always be brothers."

Sheikh Yassin patted Zayed on the back again, turned and departed as the sun finally set.

Chapter 11

The Oasis 1946

A lone figure on a camel (Wilfred Thesiger), followed by three more camel riders arrived at the oasis.

At a well, Wilfred Thesiger ordered his camel to sit and stepped over to the people milling around the well.

"Sheikh Zayed. I am looking for Sheikh Zayed."

No one answered until finally a man stepped forward and pointed east.

"He is at Al Muwaiji," he said.

Thesiger nodded and returned to his camel and left.

****

Desert Track To Al Buraimi

A convoy of clearly US Army marked military vehicles was driving along a rough desert track. On an elevated ridge, the American driver (Thomas Barger) in the lead jeep stopped and the passenger (Prince Faisal) wearing a Keffiyeh (square cotton head dress) pointed to the horizon.

"Al Buraimi Oasis. And our land."

"That may be Your Highness," replied Thomas Barger. "But the British Oil Companies and the local Bedouin still see things differently."

Prince Faisal folded his arms and an awkward silence continued.

"If it your wish Your Highness, we could camp here tonight and then tomorrow we can meet with local leaders peacefully and continue the survey work?"

Prince Faisal looked at him and then at Al Buraima Oasis in the distance.

"We will stop here tonight," said Prince Faisal.

The convoy stopped and US soldiers with machine guns and rifles got out of the trucks and started to off-load supplies to set up camp.

****

Al Muwaiji Fort, The Oasis

An older Zayed, ran out from the entrance of the fort.

"Hassa! Hassa where are you?"

He ran around the corner to see some tribesmen sitting down together. One of them hinted at a solitary figure sitting down and completely hidden.

Chapter 11

Zayed walked over slowly and pulled back the cloak to reveal Hassa has grown up into a beautiful young woman.

"That's not fair," she protested. "You cheated. Everyone wants to help you."

"Now you have to give it back," smiled Zayed.

Hassa pouted her lips and crossed her arms.

"You don't want to spend time with me unless I hide things of yours now."

"Hassa you are now a beautiful woman and I cannot. It is not proper."

Hassa frowned.

"Rules, laws, it is no fun."

Zayed frowned before he saw a glint at the side of the cloak and quickly he snatched a riding cane next to Hassa.

"Ah ha!"

"Sheikh Zayed?" a voice asked expectantly behind Zayed. He turned to see the figure of Wilfred Thesiger dressed as a traditional Bedouin. Zayed looked at him strangely.

"Why British are you dressed as a Bedu?"

"I am Wilfred Thesiger and I have come to learn about you and your customs."

Zayed

Hassa started laughing as Zayed frowned at her. He turned back to Thesiger.

"Then you are welcome as our guest, British."

****

US Military Desert Camp, Barger Tent

A US serviceman poked his head nervously into the tent of Thomas Barger.

"Sir. I think you need to get out here."

Barger opened one eye, then another before rubbing his face. He waved the serviceman away before pushing himself out of the canvas bed, before putting on his shoes and then his shirt.

Barger stepped out of his tent, still tucking in his shirt and looked around. He noticed the US Serviceman standing there without a rifle.

"Where is your rifle son?"

"That is the problem sir," the serviceman replied.

Barger then looked up and saw surrounding the whole camp was Bedu tribesman on horseback, led by Zayed, with Wilfred Thesiger on horseback watching from a distance.

"Welcome to Al Ain," smiled Zayed

Zayed then pointed to the largest tent of all, a beautiful white flowing tent at the middle of the US army tents.

"Maybe you should wake up Prince Faisal so that we may also welcome him."

There was laughter from the Bedu tribesmen on their horses. At that moment, the tent opened and Prince Faisal exited his tent in full length white and gold trimmed robes with a beautiful gold dagger held by his waist band.

"What is the meaning of this outrage? I am Prince Faisal bin Abdulaziz Al Saud and all of this is our land."

Zayed started laughing even louder, followed by the Bedu tribesmen.

"Your highness, I am Zayed bin Sultan and but a humble Bedu. I offer you my hospitality."

"You have a funny kind of hospitality taking all our guns," said Thomas Barger

"All of which will be returned to you when you leave," replied Zayed. "I assure you."

"I represent the Arabian American Oil Company and the United States Government," protested Thomas Barger

"And I thank you for coming to visit," added Zayed.

Zayed

At that moment, Ibrahim with several of his guard join the party and ride up in front of Zayed.

"I am Sheikh Ibrahim ibn Othman, the leader of the Dhawahir. What is the meaning of this? Who ordered this?"

"I did," said Zayed.

"I am the Dhawahir not you," growled Ibrahim. "You are not even the representative of the Al Bu Falah. You are an outcast -"

"I see you have much to discuss between yourselves," said Prince Faisal. "We shall meet again Your Highness. For now, we shall depart."

Prince Faisal bowed to Zayed, to the shock of Ibrahim. Zayed bowed in return. Zayed looked over to Thomas Barger.

"My men have your ammunition waiting over the other ridge."

Barger signalled to his troops.

"Pack up. We're out of here," he said.

Zayed turned his horse in a pirouette and rode away, followed by several tribesmen and Wilfred Thesiger. Ibrahim and his men were left alone as Prince Faisal ignored him and returned to his tent. The rest of the Americans also shunned him and started packing up.

Chapter 12

Abu Dhabi

Abu Dhabi and the completed Al Manhal Palace was shadowed from the sea by two British naval frigates.

Inside the palace, Samir led a British party (Sir William Hay, Hugh Rance and Patrick Stobart) was accompanied by elite British bodyguards. The entire party strode along a corridor of the Palace toward the main hall.

Inside the main hall, Shakhbut was sitting with his eye glasses reading a set of papers. Sir William Hay bounded forward with his guards around him as the palace guards inch forward nervously with their own guns. Shakhbut still does not look up.

"I don't have time for this Sheikh," growled Sir William Hay.

Shakhbut looked up shocked at the abruptness of the tone.

"I have spent a day getting here from Bahrain to sort out this issue with Al Ain," added Sir William Hay.

"I am Sheikh Shakhbut bin Sul-"

"And I am His Majesty's Representative and Governor for the whole Persian Gulf," interrupted Sir

William Hay. "So we know all that. Look, pardon the bluntness, but if you don't put a man in place at the Oasis - someone like your brother Zayed, then I am afraid the Saudis are likely to take it from you."

Hugh Rance stepped forward next to Sir William Hay.

"There are already reports out of Riyadh that Sheikh Yousuf Yassin with Prince Faisal are putting together an elite military unit trained by the Americans for an invasion of the Oasis," said Hugh Rance.

"Mohammad bin Khalifa is my representative," added Sheikh Shakhbut, "and Sheikh Ibrahim ibn Othman is the leader of the Dhawahir. There is no need -"

"You're still not getting it are you?" interrupted Sir William Hay again. "The Saudis are pumping out more than 20,000 barrels of oil a day at their Dammam oil field and within two years it will be five times that. Meanwhile, despite our best efforts, we are yet to find a drop of oil in your lands. But it is only a matter of time. The Saudis know that too. So either you make your brother the Governor of the Oasis or our ships are staying and I will be bringing a full military brigade to Abu Dhabi to provide protection of our investment."

Chapter 12

A moment of awkward silence before Shakhbut shrugged his shoulders.

****

Al Muwaiji Fort, Compound

Zayed entered the fort with his men to find Mohammad bin Khalifa was orchestrating the removal of furniture and belongings. He bowed to Mohammad, who came forward and embraced him.

"Look at you! The great Sheikh I always knew you would become."

"It was not my choice. I am sorry," said Zayed.

Hassa came outside carrying some bags and stared at Zayed and Mohammad in conversation. She caught the eye of Zayed before she moved away.

"Your brother has made a wise decision," said Mohammad. "He knows the Saudis will be back. The British have already started to form an army from all the emirates. They call them the Scouts. What do you plan to do?"

"I will call for a meeting of all the tribes first," replied Zayed. "To see if we might form a peaceful council to resolve our differences and work together against the Al Saud if they return."

Mohammad laughed.

"Good luck! God willing, if you do succeed you will be the first."

Zayed stepped closer.

"There is something else I want to ask of you," he said softly. "To ask of your permission as her father before you return to Abu Dhabi."

Mohammad smiled.

"I would be honoured to call you my son in law. And Hassa would surely approve. Although she might protest at first."

Zayed smiled as Mohammad and patted him on the back.

"Go and find her and tell her yourself."

Zayed bowed and ran off out of the fort. Mohammad turned his attention toward a set of boxes that had been placed in the compound.

"No!" screamed Hassa in the background.

Mohammad smiled to himself.

Chapter 13

Al Muwaiji Fort, Main Hall

Inside the main hall was Zayed, in a circle with ten other sheikhs and heads of tribes including Ibrahim ibn Othman, Obaid Bin Juma Al Ka'abi, Abdulla Bin Salim Al Ka'abi, Muhammad Bin Salimin Al Bu Shamis and Hasim Al-Hamini. Zayed stood up.

"We are all equals. We are all brothers, Let us speak freely without fear or favour."

Deadpan silence from the remainder of the room. Zayed cleared his throat and continued.

"Very well, let me start. How might we build a hospital and a school together, so that our children may learn and our loved ones may be healed by the best of knowledge?"

"Your brother has all the money," said Ibrahim. "We have none. How do you think such things are possible?"

"I find myself agreeing with a Sheikh of the Dhawahir that such things are not possible unless we have money from oil," said Obaid Bin Juma.

Zayed smiled.

"Why do we need money? Why is every tribe in Arabia so obsessed in the fortunes of oil, when our culture and laws from heaven give us the greatest gift of all?"

"You are not making sense," snapped Ibrahim.

"Trust my brothers. No society can survive without it. Yet, with trust, there is no obstacle that cannot be overcome."

General muffled laughter among the Sheikhs, as Zayed continued.

"Even if we have no money, I have learnt and discovered there are groups and people from around the world - doctors and teachers from western countries who will come, not for money but because they believe in God."

"Not missionaries," protested Obaid Bin Juma. "You cannot be serious?"

Zayed shook his head.

"Why must we look at people from a different culture or faith with such suspicion? Is not the first law of all Bedu that of hospitality and good faith, even unto our enemies?"

"Yes, but there are those who are less tolerant of such people and see them as a threat," added Muhammad Bin Salimin.

Chapter 13

Zayed laughed.

"Then let me ask a simple question of you all. Why is the Oasis so barren when we have more than enough water to cultivate many thousands of date palms and pasture?"

"That is easily answered," grinned Ibrahim. "Because your family controls the water rights."

Zayed looked surprised, before he saw all the sheikhs nod in agreement with Ibrahim.

"It is true," said Muhammad Bin Salimin.

"Very well then," replied Zayed. "Upon my honour and before all present, I relinquish the water rights of my family of The Oasis to this council of tribes that all may prosper and that we may transform the lives of our people."

"You can't do that," spluttered Ibrahim. "It is not possible."

"It is," smiled Zayed. "And I just did."

****

Teams of men toiled in the heat and sun, digging a channel. One of those men, covered in dirt was Zayed. They placed and bolted together pipes in the channel and then covered up the completed pipeline. At the end of the pipeline, a gate valve operating as a makeshift tap was installed. Zayed and the men turned the iron wheel on the top of the gate valve and water flowed out coursing into channels to cultivate the fields.

****

A modest building was finished and a final sign was placed on its exterior saying *Al Nahyaneia Model School*. A group applaud the opening of the school, with Zayed greeting young children who enter the school for the first time.

****

A traditional Bedu wedding was celebrated in custom, dress and song. At the centre of the celebrations were the bride (Hassa) and the groom (Zayed).

****

The Oasis, Hamasa

A convoy of former US military trucks and half tracks, now painted in the colors of Saudi Arabia trundle into the Oasis. In the lead vehicle was Turki Bin Ataishan and Captain Abdullah Ibn Na'ami. The Captain signalled for the convoy to stop, as he looked at his map.

"The airport is to the right and the main road to the Suhar and Oman was there," said the Captain.

"Good," grinned Turki Bin Ataishan. "Then seize the fort of Hamasa and this shall be our base as we cut the Oasis in half. No one gets from Abu Dhabi to Oman or back again except through our check points."

The Captain nodded and then signalled for the troops to get out of the trucks.

****

Abu Dhabi

Military trucks, guns and even artillery pieces were being off loaded from a docked transport ship as John Wilton and Martin Buckmaster were speaking with Sir William Hay.

"Say that again sir," yelled Martin Buckmaster.

"I will deal with Shakhbut," yelled Sir William Hay in reply. "Just get the troops rolling to the Oasis and Sheikh Zayed."

Zayed

Buckmaster nodded, then shook hands along with John Wilton and they turn and depart. Sir William Hay and his guards remain watching the unfolding preparations.

Chapter 14

Al Muwaiji Fort, Compound

Zayed stood on the battlements of the fort, dressed in military fatigues and traditional Bedouin head dress. Surrounding him were armed tribesmen protecting the fort. A tribesman stepped up to him.

"Your highness, the British and the Scouts will be here within the next two hours."

"When they arrive call the council of elders here," said Zayed, "so we may get the agreement of all tribal leaders."

The tribesman nodded and quickly exited.

****

Al Muwaiji Fort, Main Hall

Inside the main hall was Zayed sitting in a circle with five other sheikhs and heads of tribes.

"Where are the Ka'abi?" asked Zayed. "Where are the Dhawahir?"

Muhammad Bin Salimin arrived and nodded to Zayed.

Zayed

"The Saudi have bought the alliance of many of the Sheikhs," said Muhammad Bin Salimin. "Ibrahim is dead."

Zayed looked shocked as Hasim Al-Hamini arrived.

"Not all the tribes," grinned Hasim Al-Hamini as he bowed to Zayed. "But it is true that Ibrahim is dead. The Saudi want to start a war between the Tribes here, so they can play puppet masters and seize the whole oasis."

"Who killed Ibrahim?" asked Zayed.

The Sheikhs in the room shrug their shoulders.

"It doesn't matter," replied Muhammad Bin Salimin. "The Saudi will blame you. They know the Dhawahir hated Ibrahim and that Ibrahim hated you."

"Or they will say the Bani Ka'ab did it," said Hasim Al-Hamini.

"So long as there are guns, they will beat us by getting us to kill ourselves," said Muhammad Bin Salimin.

"Then there is only one answer to stop the madness that the Saudis are trying to start," said Zayed.

"What is that?" asked Hasim Al-Hamini.

"Don't fight," said Zayed. "Let the Saudis be the aggressors and call our men to show restraint."

Chapter 14

"How is that possible?" asked Hasim Al-Hamini. "The tribes see the Saudis and they see the bloodshed started. How then can one stop such customary calls for justice?"

"By the one who leads by example," replied Zayed. "I pledge before all of you that I will not take up a gun, nor arms ever again from this point forward. Thus, no more can any enemy seek to divide and conquer us again."

"Very noble Zayed," chuckled Muhammad Bin Salimin, "but the Saudi's don't care for such nobility, nor will the tribesmen understand."

"It is not for the Saudis or the tribesmen that I do this," said Zayed, "but to show the Americans and the British and the Europeans who are the elephants fighting over our land. If they are forced to stop such insane attempts, then maybe we have a chance of holding the Oasis."

****

The Oasis, Near Hamasa

Zayed

The British officers with the Scouts fanned out around near Hamasa, as Zayed and John Wilton and Martin Buckmaster looked on.

"Now Sheikh, if your horsemen can come from the left flank and distract the Saudis," said Martin Buckmaster, "then our people will be able to cover the centre but use our jeeps and machines guns to direct the attack from the right flank."

"I will not fight against the House of Al Saud," said Zayed.

Martin Buckmaster and John Wilton looked at each other incredulously.

"Sorry, you mean you don't want to fight, or can't fight?" asked John Wilton.

"If your men have ensured the Saudi cannot move, then I shall visit Obaid bin Juma of the Al-Ka'abi and seek him to reconsider," replied Zayed.

"Then you might want to reconsider bringing a gun Sheikh," said Martin Buckmaster sarcastically. "In case you have forgotten the Al-Ka'abi have sided with the Saudis."

"Thank you for your concern," smiled Zayed, "but I trust you shall do what is necessary, as will I."

Chapter 14

Zayed turned and walked back to a horse tied up next to military jeeps and rode away, leaving the British shaking their heads.

****

Ka'abi Village

Zayed rode alone into the Ka'abi village, while his guards remained at the entrance. Zayed rode past armed Ka'abi tribesman who look in amazement at a Sheikh riding alone through their camp. Zayed continued to where Sheikh Obaid bin Juma and Abdulla Bin Salim were standing outside a fortified building.

"Greetings Sheikh Zayed," said Obaid Bin Juma. "May I offer you the hospitality of the humble Bani Ka'abi."

Zayed acknowledged the greeting and dismounted from his horse to follow Sheikh Obaid bin Juma and Abdulla Bin Salim into the building.

Inside Sheikh Obaid bin Juma signalled for Zayed to sit down as the rest of the men sit and fresh coffee was brought out.

"I did not see you come to the council," said Zayed.

Sheikh Obaid smiled.

"Then maybe you have not heard that the Saudis have come to the Oasis?" said Obaid Bin Juma to muffled laughter around the room. "No one doubts your heart or bravery Zayed. Though you coming without men and guns was foolhardy as one of my men could have mistaken you for an enemy. However, your brother gives us no reason to support the Al Bu Falah versus the Al Saud."

"Sheikh Obaid I respect that you are thinking of your people and not how much gold the Saudis may have promised," replied Zayed. "But everything has a time and a consequence."

"Of course if you moved against your brother," said Obaid Bin Juma, "then things would be different and the Al Ka'abi would be fully behind you."

Zayed shook his head negatively.

"As you know, I made a solemn vow with my brothers never to harm one another. A man who breaks his oath or vow before heaven is not worthy to be a leader. No, I shall not move against my brother, nor shall I fight the Al Ka'abi or any of the tribes as the Al Saud and the Americans may wish."

"Then you cannot win," added Abdulla Bin Salim.

Chapter 14

"On the contrary my brothers," smiled Zayed, "the only way to win is not to be a proxy for such foreign powers but instead to force them to call for terms."

Sheikh Obaid stood up and bowed to Zayed, while the rest of the men also rise and follow the lead of Obaid.

"Then God be with you, for at this time," said Obaid Bin Juma. "The Bani Ka'abi remain allies to the House of Al Saud."

Zayed

Chapter 15

Blockade Of Hamasa

Surrounding the fort of Hamasa, were siege trenches and fortifications of the Trucial Oman Scouts, supported by British military observers. The Saudi garrison had been cut-off for two weeks, when suddenly, one of the Saudi soldiers started firing, causing the whole trapped Saudi garrison to start shooting.

Bullets started whizzing past the Scouts, taking everyone by surprise. Martin Buckmaster was sitting on a chair when the gunfire started. He quickly dropped to the ground as cover, injuring a finger in the process.

"Damn it!" he cursed.

Inching his way to the command tent, he yelled to the duty officers.

"Open fire."

The Scouts started returning fire as Martin Buckmaster then reached for a field radio.

"Bahrain, this is Owl, Over," he yelled. "Our position is under fire. Repeat we are under fire. Request immediate air support."

The Field radio crackled to life.

"Owl, this is Bahrain. Roger," came the reply. "Two birds are on their way."

"Roger that," said Martin Buckmaster as he looked over to see Zayed still standing, as the bullets continue to whizz past. "Get down," he yelled at him. "We have air support on the way to blast them out."

Zayed looked down at Martin Buckmaster and shook his head negatively.

"Tell your men to stop shooting," said Zayed sternly.

"Sheikh in case you haven't noticed we are under attack."

"Tell your men to stop shooting," replied Zayed insistently. "Tell them to stop, because if you bomb the Saudis then you give the Americans the excuse they have always wanted and been waiting for."

Martin Buckmaster looked at Zayed as a bullet zipped close by. He shook his head and waved his hand to the duty officers.

"Cease fire. Cease fire," yelled Martin Buckmaster.

The cracking of rifles slowly petered out until only a few shots coming from the Saudi lines continued and then finally stopped.

"Thank you," smiled Zayed.

Chapter 15

"One moment. I have to call off the air strike," said Martin Buckmaster as he grabbed the field radio set.

"Bahrain, this is Owl. Cancel the birds. I repeat please cancel the birds."

The radio crackled to life.

"Roger Owl. Understood. You should see them on your horizon any moment."

At that moment, two RAF jets fly at low altitude over the Hamasa position of the Saudis, followed by their engine roar, shaking the ground.

****

Al Muwaiji Fort, Main Hall

Zayed was with Martin Buckmaster in the main hall as Sheikh Abdulla Bin Salim entered with his Ka'abi tribesmen and bowed to Zayed.

"The Ka'abi pledge now their allegiance to the supreme council and not the Saudi."

Zayed grinned.

"What then of Obaid?"

Sheikh Abdulla shook his head.

"I now speak for the Bani Ka'ab, yet Obaid refuses to admit his error with the House of Al Saud."

Zayed

"Then God willing we can end this stand off and find peace," replied Zayed.

Chapter 16

Al Manhal Palace, Main Hall

Inside the main hall of the palace was Sir William Hay, accompanied by John Wilson, Martin Buckmaster and Zayed. As they watched on, Shakhbut paced the room while Samir stood quietly in the corner observing.

"The Saudis and Americans have blinked," said Sir William Hay. "The strategy of Sheikh Zayed worked. They wanted tribal civil war not a slow siege. So the United Nations has called a meeting for Geneva and has set up a five member body of Canada, Cuba, United Kingdom, Belgium and Saudi Arabia to decide on the boundaries between Abu Dhabi, Oman and Saudi Arabia."

"No foreign power has the right to decide our land," complained Shakhbut.

"Well, technically it would still have to be passed by the General Assembly," added Martin Buckmaster, "and - "

"How can Saudi Arabia possibly be an objective member of such a committee deciding a dispute of their own borders?" asked Zayed interrupting Martin Buckmaster.

Zayed

Sir William Hay shrugged his shoulders.

"All I know is that both of you have been invited to attend."

Shakhbut looked at Zayed and then back to Sir William Hay.

"I am Sheikh Shakhbut bin Sultan Al -"

"Stop, stop," said Sir William Hay interrupting Shakhbut. "Do we have to go through this dance every time? Zayed is coming and that is final. Even the Saudis agreed."

"Who?" asked Shakhbut.

"Sheikh Yousuf Yassin I believe," replied Sir William Hay. "Anyway enjoy yourself. No expense spared trip to Geneva, France and Britain on behalf of the British Government."

"Nothing is ever free when politics is involved," added Zayed.

Martin Buckmaster and John Wilton laughed, before Sir William Hay turned around and frowned at them.

****

Geneva Airport, Switzerland 1954

Chapter 16

A commercial plane came to a stop at an airport, ringed by tall snow capped mountains.

Stairs were brought to the plane, including a red carpet and as the door opened. It revealed Shakhbut wearing sunglasses in traditional white Bedu robes, followed by Zayed and then Samir and several others.

At the bottom of the steps was a welcoming party. Charles Oser stepped forward and greeted Shakhbut.

"Welcome to Switzerland Your Highness. I am Chancellor Charles Oser."

Shakhbut feigned disinterest and continued walking toward a waiting car. Zayed shook the hand of the chancellor warmly.

"Thank you for your welcome," smiled Zayed.

****

Palais Des Nations, Geneva

The car stopped at an imposing stone mausoleum looking building (Palais des Nations). Shakhbut and Zayed were escorted inside.

Inside, Shakhbut and Zayed entered into an immense meeting hall at which a table with five chairs was located. Rows of chairs surrounded the central table. As they entered Sir Reader Bullard stepped over to Shakhbut.

"Your Highness," he smiled. "I am Sir Reader Bullard, the British representative. So glad you made it."

Zayed eyeballed around the room and spotted Sheikh Yousuf Yassin across the room speaking with other delegates. Their eyes met and Sheikh Yousuf smiled and acknowledged him.

Shakhbut ignored Bullard and started to move towards the table. Sir Reader Bullard chased after him.

"No, no Sheikh, *you* sit over there," he said, pointing to chairs roped off from the main table.

Shakhbut, still wearing his sunglasses inside, stopped emotionless and continued to stare at Bullard.

"It is not my rules, sorry Your Highness, but the United Nations. You see in their eyes, Abu Dhabi is technically still under the care and protection of Her Majesty's Government."

Other official delegates started to take their place as a man (Charles De Visscher) at the table began to bang on a gavel.

"Order. This special conference will come to order."

Low mumbling from around the room, then silence.

Chapter 16

"All are gathered here today at the United Nations to seek peaceful resolution to the dispute concerning the territory known as Al Buraimi Oasis between the Kingdom of Saudi Arabia and the government of the United Kingdom. We shall begin with opening statements, starting with the Saudi Arabian delegate Sheikh Yousuf Yassin."

Sheikh Yousuf Yassin stood up and moved across to a lectern.

"Thank you Mr President. On behalf of all the peace loving people of Arabia, I trust that this committee shall make a fair and just judgement on this difficult matter against these imperial interests that deny the rights of our peop-"

"Mr President - I object," yelled Sir Reader Bullard at Charles De Visscher. "I mean, it is one thing to make a claim. But is entirely another to be lectured on history when clearly we have the Sheikh of Abu Dhabi present with us here."

Charles De Visscher nodded.

"Sheikh Yousuf Yassin, if you could please keep your statement to the facts as presented by your government and skip the emancipation speech."

Muffled laughter as Sheikh Yousuf Yassin scowled at Sir Reader Bullard.

Zayed

Chapter 17

Beau Rivage Hotel, Geneva

The beautiful facade of the Beau Rivage hotel lit by lights. Inside, Saudi guards watched every entrance as Zayed and his personal guards stepped forward. The Saudi guards moved aside and allowed Zayed to walk past where Sheikh Yousuf Yassin was waiting, at a table with another chair and no one else around.

"Thank you for agreeing to join me here."

"Custom is custom, even if we are speaking in a different world."

An attendant brought over two cups of coffee and then scampered away.

"I keep forgetting this is your first time to Europe," said Sheikh Yousuf Yassin. "Shakhbut is typical and embarrassing. But you..."

"I have read their history, replied Zayed," ignoring the slight against Shakhbut. "But until now have not had the opportunity to see it."

Zayed took a sip of his coffee.

"The British are finished," said Sheikh Yousuf Yassin. "The Americans are the new empire of the world and our allies and are addicted to oil."

Zayed

"Never underestimate the claws of an old and dying lion. Of all the animals they are the most dangerous precisely because they have nothing to lose."

Sheikh Yousuf Yassin smiled warmly, reaching over to take a sip of his coffee.

"Nor a falcon of the desert, hey Zayed?"

Zayed allowed himself the briefest of smiles as he surveyed the room and the Saudi guards. He looked over at a pillar towards the reception and then back at Sheikh Yousuf Yassin.

Standing behind the pillar at which Zayed was briefly staring, out of sight of the guards, was Samir. Hiding from view and listening to the conversation.

Sheikh Yousuf Yassin returned his coffee cup to the table and waved his finger at Zayed.

"I underestimated you at the Oasis," he smiled. "I knew you were smart - far smarter than your brother - "

The smile on the face of Zayed disappeared. Replaced at first by surprise then disgust.

"So you are the one behind everything at the Oasis! Blood has been spilt on our lands because of what you have done."

Sheikh Yousuf Yassin allowed himself a brief laugh.

Chapter 17

"Zayed, don't keep putting yourself down. Don't you see? It is all show. It is all an illusion."

Sheikh Yousuf Yassin stopped smiling as he saw Zayed remain solemn faced.

"Please don't misunderstand me, I weep...I wept for the martyrs. But we are but mice scurrying around for scraps while the cats of America and Europe decide which mouse shall live and who shall die."

"I reject your cynicism of mankind," replied Zayed. "I have even seen the good in the most dishonourable of men."

Sheikh Yousuf Yassin shook his head negatively.

"What? Do you think this United Nations Committee is going to rule in favour of your homeland Zayed? What you saw today was all for appearances. Three of the other five members of the committee have already had their votes purchased. So you can't win."

Zayed dropped his head, as Sheikh Yousuf Yassin continued.

"Why fight?" said Sheikh Yousuf Yassin softly, "when we could be the best of allies? Arabia and the whole Middle East needs heroes and I can think of none better than you. Look, if you only work with your brothers of the Al Saud, I am authorized to guarantee you thirty million dollars US, plus a fifty-fifty split on any oil."

Sheikh Yousuf Yassin waited until Zayed looked back at him.

"As for your brother, I have men already in his palace and even a man here in Geneva."

Zayed looked surprised, then shook his head.

"Oh yes!" continued Sheikh Yousuf Yassin. "Just give me the word and they will clear the path for you to become Sheikh of all of Abu Dhabi tonight."

Zayed got up from the chair and bowed to Sheikh Yousuf Yassin, before turning to walk away.

"That's it?" yelled Sheikh Yousuf Yassin, surprised at the move by Zayed. "You are just going to walk away?"

Zayed stopped and turned back to look at Sheikh Yousuf Yassin.

"A wise Bedu once told me that the desert will strip a man of everything until finally all he has left is his character."

Zayed then departed.

"Fine then," yelled Sheikh Yousuf Yassin. "Keep your precious honour. Turn your back on reality and keep dreaming. No one remembers a dreamer anyway."

Chapter 17

Zayed

Chapter 18

Palais Des Nations, Main Hall

There was an added frostiness in the air, as deliberations continued in the main call. Charles De Visscher was at the lecturn.

"Today, we shall begin hearing testimonies from witnesses in relation to this dispute beginning with Sheikh Shakhbut bin Sultan Al Nahyan -

"Point of order Mr President," interrupted Sheikh Yousuf Yassin.

"Yes, what is it Sheikh Yassin?" asked Charles De Visscher.

"Have we not already heard the substance of the dispute from all those official delegates possessing sovereign powers to act? While I respect my Al Bu Falah brothers, they relinquished their sovereign rights to the United Kingdom and we have already heard from the delegate of Her Majesty. Why then cannot we vote now?"

"As a matter of good faith and due process," replied Charles De Visscher, "we really should permit -"

"No more mumbo jumbo Mr President," growled Sheikh Yousuf Yassin, interrupting Charles De

Visscher again. "I only care for what the law says and -
"

"Yes Mr President I agree with Sheikh Yousuf Yassin about the law," said Zayed in a loud booming voice.

The whole room turned and looked at Zayed who had stood up. Zayed then walked toward the main delegate table. Charles De Visscher put his hand up.

"Ah Sheikh Zayed," replied Charles De Visscher, "I am sorry but - "

Sheikh Yousuf Yassin put up his hand to silence Charles De Visscher.

"Let him speak."

Zayed bowed to Sheikh Yousuf Yassin.

"What is the law of civilised society Mr President?" asked Zayed. "Is it not the same for all people of respect and learning, that none are above the law and all are equal before the law?"

"Ah yes, I guess it is," said Charles De Visscher. "You are correct, but this -"

"Yes, I am sorry, we are speaking about whether all of you here have the right to determine the future of the lands of my people," smiled Zayed. "Because of a treaty signed in 1853 that continued to be honoured by my grandfather Zayed bin Sultan and with all the Bani

Yas with the British that did not cede sovereignty, or any rights, because there was no war or conquest."

"Sheikh Zayed, the terms and rules of the United Nations do not permit us to debate such history," added Charles De Visscher, "and whether - "

"Yes, please I apologise for interrupting again," replied Zayed after interrupting Charles De Visscher for the second time. "You are right. We are just talking about the law, isn't that correct Sheikh Yousuf Yassin?"

Sheikh Yousuf Yassin looked surprised, then composed himself.

"Precisely," responded Sheikh Yousuf Yassin.

"So please tell me Sheikh Yousuf what you know of the rules of this committee if any party on the committee was found to be acting in bad faith and with unclean hands?" asked Zayed.

"Sheikh Zayed," blurted Charles De Visscher, "now I must remind you that you are a guest and -"

"Like a bribe!" continued Zayed. "Would that not be the end of their career and a disgrace to their country?"

There was uproar among the observers and even delegates, causing Charles De Visscher to keep banging his gavel.

"Order. The meeting will come to order."

Zayed

"Mr President," said Sir Reader Bullard. "I must inform you, that as of this moment, I formally resign from this committee, effective immediately."

More uproar as Zayed and Sheikh Yousuf Yassin locked eyes. Charles De Visscher kept banging his gavel.

"Order. Order," yelled Charles De Visscher to no avail. "I too feel my position as President of the committee is untenable and also I therefore resign, effective immediately."

Now the whole room was in full uproar at the collapse of the committee, as Sheikh Yousuf Yassin allowed himself a brief smile before breaking eye contact with Zayed.

****

Palais Des Nations, Entrance Hall

Shakhbut and Zayed followed the other delegates and attendees into the entrance hall, where Sheikh Yousuf Yassin and his staff were standing to the side, in wait.

"You may have won here Zayed, but it is too late for the Oasis," grinned Sheikh Yousuf Yassin. "I have

Chapter 18

already ordered our army to complete the capture of Al Ain and end this charade."

Zayed smiled.

"Why are you smiling?" asked Sheikh Yousuf Yassin.

"Because this morning, the British radioed that their forces at the Oasis, supported by the united tribes of the Bani Yas and the Dhawahir and even the Bani Ka'ab, overwhelmed your forces," said Zayed. "Your forces have surrendered."

****

In Hamasa a mass army of military uniformed members of the Trucial Oman Scouts and Bedu tribesmen overwhelmed the Saudi garrison.

Some Saudi forces try and fight back including Captain Abdullah ibn Na'ami, who was shot by the troops and the final Saudi forces surrendered.

****

Sheikh Yousuf Yassin looked directly at Zayed, who did not blink, then started laughing.

Zayed

"You have always been a daydreamer Zayed. Very funny. If we have lost the Oasis then I would have known about it. The Americans would have told me."

Just then a nervous looking aide next to the Sheikh with his arm shaking handed a telex message to Sheikh Yousuf Yassin. The Sheikh read it then glared at Zayed.

"It is not over," growled Sheikh Yousuf Yassin, before spinning around and stomping out of the hall.

Chapter 19

Abu Dhabi

A commercial plane came to a stop at the airstrip of Abu Dhabi. A rickety set of stairs was pushed over as the door to the plane opened. Shakhbut followed by Zayed and then Samir stepped off the plane.

As soon as he was on the ground, Shakhbut and several guards stepped away to a waiting vehicle without a word.

"We will drive you back to the Oasis," said Samir.

Zayed continued to watch Shakhbut as he got into the back of the other car and never once glanced back. Zayed, then turned to Samir and followed him with two other guards to another vehicle.

****

Road To Oasis

Zayed's car was driving along the road to the Oasis. He was sitting in the back with a guard, with Samir seated in the front passenger seat.

Zayed

"You know, it is strange that Shakhbut did not say a single word to me on the final day of the conference," said Zayed.

Samir shrugged his shoulders and kept looking ahead.

"It is as almost as if he was told something," added Zayed.

Samir turned around and smiles at Zayed.

"You know your brother. He is always a pessimist and worrying about people scurrying about," replied Samir.

"Funny, that sounds just like what someone else said to me."

Samir quickly glanced to the guard sitting next to Zayed who produced a dagger and in an instant, Zayed, grabbed the arm of the guard and pushed the knife back. In the struggle, Samir produced a gun and took aim at Zayed in the back seat.

In an instant, Zayed let the force of the guard propel himself to his side of the back seat and turned him around to use his body to shield him from the gun, causing Samir to shoot the guard. Zayed then pushed the dying guard still holding the knife into the back of the driver, causing him to lose control.

Chapter 19

The vehicle rolled several times on the road, before coming to a dusty stop upside down. The lights were still on and the engine was smoking. Slowly, Zayed, with a cut on his head, dragged himself out of one side of the car as Samir pulled himself out of the other and start limping away.

The driver had been thrown out onto the road and was convulsing and moaning in the last moments of his life.

"Help me.." said the dying driver.

Zayed kneels down and reaches back into the wrecked car and retrieved the revolver dropped by Samir. He moved back to the Driver, aimed the revolver and fires one shot at him at close range. The moaning stopped. Zayed then kneeled down and put his hand over the eyelids of the dead driver.

Zayed got up, wiping his own blood from his forehead and stepped around the vehicle and aimed the revolver towards Samir who had failed to limp too far. He fired one more shot and Samir froze and put his hands up.

"Stop!" yelled Zayed. "Turn around!"

Zayed then limped up to Samir who had turned around in front of the lights of the vehicle. The engine of the overturned vehicle now on fire.

Zayed

"So it was you that Yassin was talking about," said Zayed.

"What does it matter?" groaned Samir. "You are going to kill me anyway."

"I haven't decided, yet," replied Zayed. "I have a few more things I need answered first, starting with wh-

"Why did I do it?" interrupted Samir. "Why did I take the money from Yassin? The same as any man would do for his family, to provi-"

"But without honour Samir. You have nothing."

Samir started laughing until his injuries started hurting and he dropped his arms to hold his ribs. Zayed used the revolver to motion for Samir to put his hands up again.

At that moment, the engine to the vehicle exploded and both men were briefly thrown to the ground. Zayed picked himself up and then dragged Samir up from the ground.

"What do we do now?" asked Samir. "How do we get back."

Zayed motioned for Samir to put his hands up as the car was now fully alight.

"Start walking."

Chapter 19

Zayed motioned for Samir, still with his hands up to start walking in the direction back to Abu Dhabi.

Zayed

Chapter 20

Al Manhal Palace, Main Hall

Shakhbut was sitting, reading with his glasses, when Samir entered, bruised and limping slightly. Shakhbut looked up and was taken back by his appearance.

"Where have you been? Is it done?"

Before Samir could even open his mouth, Sir William Hay, accompanied by John Wilson, Martin Buckmaster and a troop of British marines entered the room and surprised the guards.

"Not quite," said Sir William Hay.

The marines disarmed the guards as Shakhbut shook his head and sat back down in his chair, just as Zayed, the head wound stitched, entered the room.

"Why brother?" asked Zayed. "You swore a solemn oath. We all swore an oath before our mother and the tribes."

Shakhbut glared back defiantly.

"Samir told me of your meeting with Yassin and the Al Saud."

Zayed shook his head as he looked over at Samir, now under guard by the marines.

Zayed

"Samir betrayed you. He was the one working for the Al Saud."

Shakhbut looked over at Samir stunned.

"Is this true?"

Samir started crying.

"Please forgive me."

"I did not know brother," said Shakhbut as he started to walk toward Zayed. "I would never -"

Just as they embrace, Shakhbut reached down and grabs the knife from the belt of Zayed and lunged at Samir, thrusting the knife deep into the chest of Samir who screamed. In a second, the British marines grab Shakhbut and hold him back. Samir collapsed to the ground mortally wounded.

****

Abu Dhabi Airstrip

Zayed was standing with several guards next to a jet plane being loaded for take-off, when a car arrived. Shakhbut stepped out of the car and then walked over toward the plane and to where Zayed was standing. Shakhbut bowed his head.

Chapter 20

"Brother, I only tried to do what is best for our family."

The jet started to warm up its engines.

"I know," smiled Zayed. "And if God did not want it to be so, then none of these miracles would have happened."

Zayed embraced his brother. "But now we must become more than what we once were."

Shakhbut bowed his head, turned and steps onto the plane. The door closed as the engines increase in pitch and volume. Zayed stepped back.

Shakhbut sat back in his seat, staring out through the window at Zayed and the sparse airport.

Zayed watched the plane of Shakhbut take off into the afternoon light.

He then turned and stared back toward the coast line and the solitary structure of the Al Manhal Palace rising above the skyline.

"Every change is difficult. Every time a new leader is chosen is a test of the resolve of the people for peace."

****

Zayed

The British and French did finally discover oil just off our shore in huge quantities. Despite such new found wealth and the politics of such power, the transition to the best use of such gifts took time.

Yet we did not go to war with the Al Saud. And wiser and more experienced heads were able to find common ground and common respect.

A Great Bedu leader once taught me, to never surrender your dreams or give up on your faith in heaven. For what may seem but the dream of a child, may one day become the legacy for generations to come.